Melissa Senate has written many novels for Mills & Boon and other publishers, including her debut, *See Jane Date*, which was made into a TV movie. She also wrote seven books for Mills & Boon True Love line under the pen name Meg Maxwell. Her novels have been published in over twenty-five countries. Melissa lives on the coast of Maine with her teenaged son, their sweet beagle, Lemon, and a lap cat named Cleo. For more information, please visit her website, www.melissasenate.com.

THE BABY SWITCH!

MELISSA SENATE

Printed and bound in Spain
by CPI, Barcelona

MILLS & BOON

First Published in Great Britain 2018
by Mills & Boon, an imprint of HarperCollins*Publishers*
1 London Bridge Street, London, SE1 9GF

The Baby Switch! © 2018 Melissa Senate

ISBN: 978-0-263-26488-3

38-0418

Dedicated to the one,
the only Gail Chasan,
editor extraordinaire.
I can't thank you enough for everything.

Chapter One

Liam Mercer's agenda for Friday, April 14:

*Negotiate 2.4 million-dollar acquisition of Kenyon Corp.

*Take six-month-old son for first haircut at Kidz Kutz, where apparently there was a baby seat in the shape of a choo-choo train, and a puppet show video to distract criers.

*Preside over four meetings, sign countless documents, approve hiring of VP in New Business Development, prepare quarterly report for board of directors.

*Repair lifetime rift between his father, the imperious Harrington Mercer, and his I'll-do-what-I-want-it's-my-life younger brother over the weekly family dinner tonight at the Mercer ranch.

Just another Friday. Well, except for the haircut. That was new. Liam loved firsts when it came to Alexander and noted them all in the leather-bound baby book his cousin Clara had given him, along with a seven-foot-tall stuffed giraffe, the day after Alexander was born. The first notation of the first first: at barely a half hour old, Alexander West Mercer wrapped his tiny fist around Liam's pinky. Every worry and fear that a single, twenty-eight-year-old corporate president who'd had no idea he was even going to be a father could actually raise a helpless living creature on his own, fell away. Of course, every one of those worries returned two seconds later, but his heart had been swiped by the little guy. A love he'd never felt before had come bursting out of Liam's chest. And that was that.

He shifted Alexander in his arm, nudged the heavy baby bag higher up on his other shoulder and pulled open the door to Mercer Industries. Despite the fleece jacket with its bear-ears hood covering his son's dark hair, the silky wisps were getting so unruly they were peeking out. The plan was to knock off the acquisition, deal with two of the meetings, then slip away at lunchtime to Kidz Kutz and be ready with his camera.

"There's Wyoming's luckiest baby!"

Liam turned around in the reception area. Clara, his favorite cousin and right-hand woman, VP of Mercer Industries, bent forward to coo at Alexander. As it was just before nine o'clock, employees began streaming through the doors, smiling at Alexander as they passed through to the elevator bank.

Clara gave the baby a little tap on the nose. "Yup,

luckiest. Millionaire at birth, gorgeous gray-blue eyes and the Mercer dimple and a doting extended family, including myself. Oh, and let's not forget a daddy who refuses to hire a nanny and instead keeps him close by at the cushy company day care and visits twice a day."

"Three times, actually," Liam said. He couldn't spend enough time with his son.

And at least it was Friday. Even though Liam always had work crowding his weekend, he was looking forward to his plans to take Alexander on a hike up Wedlock Creek Mountain to see the huge Cottonwoods. Alexander would watch the scenery from his perch in the backpack carrier, one of the zillion baby gifts he'd received from family and friends and coworkers in total shock that Liam Mercer, who wasn't exactly a playboy but lived for work, had become a father.

After the hike it would be library time, where he'd sack out on the huge bean bags dotting the children's room and read Alexander's favorite book three times, the one with the talking pear named Joe. On Sunday they'd head to his family's ranch, a huge spread with a small petting zoo that his father had created just for Alexander. He was a good eight months away from feeding a goat pellets from his hand, but his dad wanted the zoo in place "because clearly Alexander is advanced." His father was way over-the-top when it came to Alexander, but Liam had to admit the grandfatherly pride was touching. Especially from Harrington Mercer.

Liam's phone buzzed in his pocket, as it had been doing for the past half hour, par for the course for the president of Mercer Industries. But he couldn't reach his phone with Alexander in one arm and his baby bag in the other. "Hold him for a sec, will you, Clara?"

She wrinkled her nose. "And risk baby spit-up on my dress for the big meeting with Kenyon Corp? No way." She did a few rounds of peekaboo, covering her face and opening her hands to reveal a big smile to a rapt Alexander. "Peekaboo, I see you! And I swear I love you even if I won't risk what happened last month at your grandmother's birthday dinner. Oh, yeah. I know you remember, drool-boy." She blew a kiss at Alexander, then headed through the frosted-glass double doors on her very high heels.

Liam rolled his eyes with a smile. Six months and a day ago, he'd been the same way. He'd no sooner go near a sticky baby than pet an animal who'd get white hairs on his Hugo Boss suit. But six months and a day ago, Liam hadn't even known he was about to become a father.

Life could change just like that. And had.

And now Liam knew how wrong he and Clara were about their expensive clothes and perfect hair. Spit-up didn't bother him at all. Changing diapers—no problem. Alexander's new favorite solid food—Toasty Os cereal—thrown at his hair with a giggle? Good arm, kid. It was amazing how Liam had changed in six months because of one tiny baby. His baby.

And Clara was wrong about something else. Alexander wasn't the luckiest baby in Wyoming. He didn't have everything.

He didn't have a mother.

After the shock had worn off, when Liam had stepped into his new role as someone's father, when he'd sit with Alexander in the middle of the night in the rocking chair in the nursery, feeding him a bottle, holding him, rocking him, breathing in the baby-shampoo scent of him, staring at every beautiful bit of him, all Liam could really focus on was the fact that his baby's mother had died during childbirth, that this innocent child in his arms was motherless.

Liam was doing okay as a father, maybe even better than okay. It had been some learning curve. He'd forced himself to take two weeks off from the office, hired a baby nurse to teach him the ropes, which had involved waking up every few hours, warming baby bottles, changing diapers, acquainting himself with ointments and lotions and baby bathtubs, and figuring out which cry meant hungry or diaper rash or gas or *pick me up.* Now, six months later, he basically knew what he was doing. But no matter that Liam was there, really there, he was no substitute for a mother.

The problem with finding a mother for his son was that Liam wasn't looking for a *wife.*

"There's our little heir," came the voice of Harrington Mercer. The fifty-eight-year-old CEO took Alexander and held him high in the air, his own expensive suit be damned. "Good, Alexander, you're all ready for a day of soaking up the corporate culture. You'll intern here through college, then get your MBA, and you'll be in line to take over Mercer Industries, just like your father and your grandfather did from great-granddad Wilton Mercer."

Liam mentally shook his head. "Dad, he's six months old. Let's get him sleeping through the night before he starts as a junior analyst at MI."

His father waved his hand in the air. "Never too soon to immerse the heir in the learning process. Anyone knows that, it's you, Liam. Heck, you grew up in this building." His dad smiled and kissed Alexander on the cheek. "Oh, I have a little present for you, Alexander." He set his briefcase on the reception desk and opened it, and pulled out a tiny brown Stetson. "There. We may be businessmen, but we're Wyoming men and cowboys at heart."

Harrington Mercer took off Alexander's hood and settled the little hat, lined with fleece, on his head, nodded approvingly, then handed him back to Liam and headed through the double doors.

"One minute I don't understand your grandfather at all," he whispered to Alexander. "And the next, I want to hug him. People are complicated. Life lesson one thousand five."

Alexander smiled and reached out to squeeze Liam's chin.

"You know what's not complicated?" Liam whispered as he shifted his son to push open the door. "How much I love you."

Liam took the elevator to the fourth floor, which held the company's health club, cafeteria and the day care, using his key card to open the door to the day care center. The main room, separated from the door with a white picket fence-gate decorated with grass and trees and flowers, was for the toddlers and pre-school-age kids. Liam waved at one of the teachers, then headed into the nursery for babies under fourteen months. The room, with its pale blue walls bordered with smiling cartoon animals, was cozy with its decor and baby gear, the play mats and bouncers and bassinets with little spinning mobiles playing lullabies. Two babies were already there, having tummy time on the thickly padded mats. There were seven babies currently, ranging in age from three to twelve months.

"Morning, Liam," the nursery director said with a smile. "And good morning, Alexander. I like your hat."

Liam signed in his son and handed him over, always feeling like he was handing over a piece of his heart. Another employee came in with her four-month-old and stood for a while by the window, nuzzling her little daughter's cheek before finally giving her to the director with a wistful smile.

I know how you feel, he thought, staring at his baby son. *It's so hard to say goodbye, even for a few hours*.

The day care center had been started almost sixty years ago by his grandmother, Alexandra Mercer, for whom Alexander was named. Back then, when the brilliant businesswoman, then president of Mercer Industries, became a mother, she'd insisted that her husband, Wilton, the CEO, agree to open a day care center on site for all employees. She'd hired the best nannies in Wedlock Creek to staff the new corporate day care and told off anyone who dared say that she should be at home, raising her child herself. Back then, not many employees partook in the service offered. But now, with women comprising over half the employees at MI, the day care center was almost always filled to capacity. Knowing their babies and toddlers and preschoolers were well taken care of just an elevator ride away made for happier, more productive employees. Liam could attest to that firsthand.

He kneeled down on Alexander's play mat and pulled out his phone to take a photo of Alexander in his cowboy hat, noticing an unfamiliar number on the screen. The same number had called three times in the past half hour. As he snapped the photo of Alexander, the phone buzzed again.

"Can I throw this thing out the window?" Liam asked the director.

She laughed. "You go ahead—answer it, I mean. We'll take good care of Alexander."

Liam smiled and nodded. "See you in a few hours for lunch and a haircut, cowboy," he said to Alexander, then finally answered the call on his way out the door.

"Liam Mercer," he said.

"Oh, thank goodness we finally reached you," a female voice said. "Mr. Mercer, my name is Anne Parcells. I'm the administrator of the Wedlock Creek Clinic. We need you to come to the clinic right away and to bring the minor child, Alexander West Mercer, and your attorney."

He froze. The minor child? His attorney? What the hell was this?

Liam frowned. "What's this about?"

"We'll discuss everything at the meeting," Parcells said. "If you can get here by 9:15, that would be appreciated. The others will be here by then, as well."

"The others?"

She didn't respond to that. "Can we expect you by 9:15, Mr. Mercer? Please come to my office, two doors from the main entrance."

Liam glanced at his watch. It was 8:55. "I'll be there."

There for what, though? Alexander was born in the Wedlock Creek Clinic. If the administrator was referring to his son as "the minor child" and talking attorneys, there was probably some kind of liability issue regarding the night he was born. A class action lawsuit, maybe. Liam closed his eyes for a second as memories of the snowstorm came back, memories he'd tried to block. Alexander's mother phoning him, a desperation in Liza Harwood's voice he'd never heard before, not that he'd known her very long.

Liam, there's no time for explanations. I'm nine months pregnant with your baby and in labor. I should have told you before but I'm telling you now. I'm on my way to the clinic. The snowstorm is so bad. If anything happens to me, I left you a letter...

Nine months pregnant with his baby. And something had happened to Liza.

Most of Wedlock Creek had lost power that night, and the clinic's backup generator had blinked out twice. There had been so many accidents in town—from tree limbs falling on houses to car wrecks and pickups in ditches. Liza had made it to the clinic in one piece but had not survived childbirth. A tragedy that had had nothing to do with the storm or the clinic.

Liam closed his eyes again, then shook his head to clear it. He had to call his lawyer, reorganize his morning and get to the clinic.

He headed back inside the nursery for Alexander. At least he'd have some unexpected extra time with his son this morning, after all.

Shelby Ingalls sat in an uncomfortable folding chair in the Wedlock Creek Clinic's administrator's office, holding her baby son against her chest in the sling he was fast asleep in. She glanced at the doorway, hoping the woman would come back and get this meeting—whatever it was about—underway. Opening time at Treasures, her secondhand shop, was ten o'clock, and

Shelby wanted to display the gorgeous antique frames she'd found at an estate sale the other day and the cute new mugs with napping beagles on them. She knew several of her regular customers would love those.

She'd been about to head down to the shop when Anne Parcells had called, asking Shelby to come in and "bring the minor child" and her attorney. The phrasing and the word *attorney* had freaked her out, but the administrator had refused to say anything else. Shelby had been so panicked that it had something to do with Shane's blood test, that he was terribly ill after all. A week ago she'd brought him into the clinic for a stomach virus and had been waiting for the results, which she'd been sure would reveal nothing since the virus had cleared up and Shane was back to his regular happy little self. But despite the director assuring her that Shane was perfectly healthy, Anne Parcells again requested that she come immediately to the clinic— and to bring an attorney.

First of all, Shelby didn't have an attorney, and despite the size of her extended family, there wasn't a lawyer in the bunch. Nor did she want this weird request from the director to become family fodder until she herself knew what it was all about. Her sister, her mother, her aunt Cheyenne and a bunch of cousins would be crowded in the back of this room if she'd let anyone know. So she'd called her sister, Norah, who despite being a chatterbox who knew everyone and all the town gossip, could keep a secret like no one else. Turned out, Norah was newly dating a lawyer, an ambulance-chasing type, and so much of a shark that she was thinking of breaking up with him because of it. A few minutes later Norah had called back and assured Shelby that David Dirk, attorney at law, would meet Shelby at the clinic by 9:10—and that the meeting was probably about some lawsuit from the night Shane was born because of the storm and the generator failing twice. In any case, Norah had promised to keep mum about the meeting and texted:

I get to know what it's about, though, right? Call me the minute you're out of there!

Shane stirred against her chest, and she glanced down at her dear little son, caressing his fine brown wisps. A moment later, an attractive guy in his early thirties appeared in the doorway. He had a baby face and tousled hair, but he wore a sharp suit and had intelligent eyes behind black-framed glasses. Not Norah's typical brawny rancher type.

"David Dirk," he said, extending a hand and sitting down beside her. "When the administrator arrives and says her spiel, don't comment, don't agree to anything, don't answer anything with yes or no. In fact, let me speak for you."

"I always speak for myself," Shelby said. "But I'll listen to your advice and we'll go from there."

Before he could respond, two other men appeared in the doorway, and at the sight of the one holding a baby wearing a brown cowboy hat, Shelby almost gasped.

She knew him. Well, she'd seen him before. And she'd never forget his face. Not just because he was incredibly good-looking—six feet one or two and leanly muscular with thick, dark hair and gorgeous blue eyes, a dimple curving into the left side of his mouth. It was that she'd never forget the combination of fear and worry that had been etched into his features, in those eyes. The night she'd given birth, he'd been sitting in the crowded waiting room of this clinic, his head in hands, when the ambulance EMTs had rushed her inside on a gurney. He'd looked up and they'd locked eyes, and despite the fact that she was already in labor and breathing and moaning like a madwoman, the complex combination of emotions on the man's face had so arrested her that for one single moment, she'd been aware of nothing else but him. Given the pain she was in, the contractions coming just a minute and a half apart, that was saying something. A second later she'd let out a wail that had even her covering her ears, and the EMT had hurried into a delivery room.

She'd wondered about the man in the waiting room ever since, if whomever he'd been waiting on had been okay. There had been one hell of a storm that night, so much blinding snow that a ten-minute ride to the clinic from her apartment above her shop had taken almost an hour.

Because she was now staring at the man with the baby cowboy, he glanced at her, and she could see he was trying to place her.

"Good morning," a woman said, her voice serious as she appeared behind the two men in the doorway. "I'm Anne Parcells, administrator of the Wedlock Creek Clinic. All parties are here so let's begin. Please," she said, gesturing for the men to enter and to sit in the two chairs positioned to the left of her desk. Shelby and her attorney were seated to the right. "Thank you for coming, Ms. Ingalls and Mr. Mercer." Introductions were made between attorneys and parties, the door was closed and everyone was now seated.

Please get to the lawsuit or whatever this is about so that I can get back to the store, Shelby thought. Three of her favorite regular customers, the elderly Minnow sisters, came in every Friday morning at the shop's opening time of ten o'clock to see what she might have added to the shop for the weekend rush. She hated to keep them and any new customers waiting. Wedlock Creek was a small town, but had its own rodeo on the outskirts and a bustling downtown because of it, so folks came from all over the county to enjoy a bit of the Wild West, then walk the mile-long Main Street with its shops and restaurants and movie theater with the reclining seats. Business was semi-booming.

The administrator cleared her throat, her expression almost grim. Shelby felt for the woman. The Wedlock Creek Clinic, a nonprofit that included an urgent care center, was a godsend for so many in the county, since the county hospital was forty-five minutes away. A lawsuit had the potential to close the clinic.

"I'm going to just say this outright," Anne said, looking up from some paperwork. "A week ago, Ms. Ingalls—" she gestured to Shelby "—brought her six-month-old son, Shane, to the clinic with a stomach virus. A standard blood test was run. This morning our lab returned the results, noting a discrepancy with Ms. Ingalls's blood type and Shane Ingalls's blood type."

A discrepancy? Huh? Shelby leaned forward a bit, staring at the woman, who glanced at her for a moment, the expression in her eyes so compassionate that the hairs rose on the back of Shelby's neck.

Anne Parcells looked down at the papers in her hands, then back up. "Based on the results, it would be impossible for Ms. Ingalls to be Shane's biological mother."

What the ever-loving hell? Shelby bolted up, her arms around Shane in the sling. "That's impossible! Of course he's my son! I gave birth to him!"

The administrator's expression turned grim again. "The test was run three times. I'm afraid that Shane Ingalls cannot be your biological son, Ms. Ingalls."

Shelby's legs shook and she dropped down on her chair, her head spinning. She tried to make sense of the words. *Not your son. Discrepancy. Impossible.*

This had to be a mistake—that was the only explanation. Of course Shane was her son!

Dimly, she could hear her sister-appointed lawyer requesting to see the paperwork, the ruffling of sheaves of paper as Anne handed over the stack and David Dirk studied them, flipping through the various documents.

"Jesus," David mutter-whispered.

Shelby closed her eyes, trying to keep hold of herself despite the feeling coming over her that she was going to black out. She felt herself wobble a bit and grabbed David's chair to steady herself.

He put a bracing arm around her. "We'll have your and Shane's blood drawn again and retested in a different lab," he said.

She sucked in a breath and nodded. Yes. Redone. A different lab. It was a mistake. Just a mistake. The results would prove she was Shane's mother. She was!

"Excuse me," Liam Mercer's lawyer said, darting a compassionate glance at Shelby. "But what does this have to do with my client?"

The administrator took a deep breath. "Based on the results and a discussion with a night-shift nurse who retired three months ago, we believe your babies—Shane Ingalls and Alexander Mercer—born within minutes of each other in the early-morning hours of November 5, were accidentally switched at birth."

Chapter Two

Shelby gasped.

"That's impossible," Liam Mercer said, his gaze narrowed on the administrator, then on Shelby. "Come on."

The woman glanced from Shelby to Liam, then said, "In the chaos of the storm, the nurse didn't follow procedure to secure an identifying bracelet around the male babies until the generator kicked back in. She was positive she'd put Ms. Ingalls's baby in the left bassinet and Ms. Harwood's in the right. But because we now know that Shane Ingalls can't be the child Shelby gave birth to, she thinks she must have made a mistake."

Liam stood up, tightening his hold on the baby in his arms. "That's ridiculous. Like Mr. Dirk said, the blood test results are a mistake. A mislabeled vial, and voilà, mother and baby are suddenly not related. There was no switching of babies."

"Mr. Mercer," Anne Parcells said. "I wish that were the case. However, given that the generator failed at precisely the time when both babies were taken, within minutes of each other, to the pediatric clinic to be weighed and measured and cleaned up, it's entirely possible that the nurse accidentally switched the babies. I also wish that the blood type issue could be a mistake, but Ms. Ingalls's blood was drawn twice on prior visits to the clinic during prenatal care—and documented, of course. Her blood type is not compatible with Shane's."

Oh, God. There went her last hope.

"*Entirely possible* isn't good enough," Liam said, his voice ice-cold. "Either the nurse did switch the babies or she didn't. If you don't know for sure, then…" He shook his head, then stared at Anne Parcells. "Wait a minute. Alexander was born here, so you must have his blood type on record and his mother's. Are they compatible? I'm sure they are."

The administrator nodded. "Alexander's blood type, one of the most common, is a match for Liza Harwood's. However, it's also a match for Ms. Ingalls. Which leads to next steps. DNA tests must be conducted."

"There," Liam said, "Alexander's blood type is compatible with his mother's. And mine, I'm sure. He's my son."

"You visited the urgent care center twice in the past five years, Mr. Mercer. Your blood type is on record. Your blood type is compatible with Alexander's, as well."

The relief that crossed Liam's face almost had Shelby happy for him. But she was barely hanging on.

"This is all some mix-up with Ms. Ingalls and her son's blood type but it has nothing to do with me." He looked over at Shelby then, his expression a mix of confusion and worry. Just like the night she'd first seen him. "I don't mean to sound cavalier at your expense, Ms. Ingalls, but this is a mistake," he said to her. "It has to be."

"He's right!" Shelby shouted, panic and bile rising. "It's *all* a mistake. It has to be a mistake!"

"There were four babies born the night of November 5," the director said. "Two boys and two girls. If there was a switch, it was between Shane Ingalls and Alexander Mercer."

The lawyers began talking, but Shelby's ears felt like they were stuffed with cotton. As Liam began pacing, she glanced at the baby in his arms—and gasped.

"What?" Liam asked, freezing, his gaze narrowed on her again.

"The little birthmark on his ear," she whispered, standing up. "I have it, too. So does my grandmother." Norah didn't have it. Her mother didn't have it. But Shelby *did*.

Everyone peered at the tiny reddish-brown spot on the baby's earlobe. Then at Shelby's ear.

"Oh, for God's sake. It's nothing," Liam said, shifting Alexander in his arms so that he was out of view. "It's a mark that will fade away."

Shelby's legs shook to the point that she dropped back down in her chair. She stared at Shane's dark hair, so unlike her own, which was blond. But Shane's father, a bronc rider she'd foolishly married after a whirlwind courtship and who'd left town with another woman the moment Shelby told him she was pregnant, had Shane's same dark hair. He had blue eyes, too, just like Shane.

But the baby in Liam Mercer's arms was also dark-haired. Also blue-eyed.

In fact, the babies looked a lot alike, except for the shapes of their faces, and Shane's features were a little sharper than Alexander's. Did Shane look like Liam Mercer? Okay, yes. But he also looked a little like Shelby. Even if no one ever commented on that. *He must look like his daddy*, she'd heard someone say a time or two as they'd peered in Shane's stroller, then at her.

She suddenly felt dizzy and put her hand on her lawyer's chair to brace herself again. Oh, God. Oh, God. Oh, God. This could not be happening.

It was a mistake. Shane was her son.

Liam's lawyer also flipped through the paperwork, then looked up. "As there's no reason to believe that Alexander West Mercer is not my client's biological child, based on blood type, we'll await DNA results before any further discussion."

Shelby's lawyer nodded. "We'll have Shelby's and Shane's blood tested for type at a separate facility. Until those results come in, we also will proceed with the understanding that Shane Ingalls is Shelby Ingalls's biological child.

Thank God Norah was dating a lawyer. Shelby's mind was in such a state that she'd never have thought of that.

"If that is agreeable to both parties," the administrator said. "Of course I'll need you both to sign some documents."

Shelby stared down at Shane, the voices retreating as everything inside her went numb. She held him as close as she could without squeezing him. He was her son.

"I saw you," Liam said, a reluctant awareness edging his deep voice.

Shelby looked up. Liam was standing in front of her and staring at her.

"The night Alexander was born," he said. "I was in the waiting room and you were suddenly wheeled in, but another gurney was blocking the doorway. I was afraid you'd deliver right there in front of me."

"I remember," she said. *The sight of you, the way our eyes met, gave me something concrete to focus on.*

"I'd like to confer with my client," Liam's attorney said.

"As would I," Shelby's lawyer said.

Liam and his lawyer stepped to the back of the room. Shelby and hers stayed at the front.

"Until we have your blood tested again, Shane is your son same as he was a half hour ago," David said. "Even if the results indicate that you and Shane can't be biologically related, operate under the assumption that he is your child under the law until the DNA tests are in."

He is. He is my son! But she heard herself ask the impossible. "What if he isn't?" she said, her voice strangled on a sob. "What if he's not my son?"

"Then the four of us will meet again, Shelby. But until we know for sure, don't agree to anything Mercer or his attorney asks of you and for God's sake, don't sign anything. Do you hear me?"

She nodded. "I hear you."

The administrator took Shelby and Liam and their attorneys into a room, explained in detail how the DNA test worked, then had a technician swab the inside of their mouths and draw blood for good measure, vials labeled with their names. In addition to their attorneys, two techs served as witnesses and the entire process was videotaped to assure all was handled correctly. Shelby and Liam both watched, eagle-eyed, as the swabs and vials were sealed into separate bags.

"I'll also have my and Shane's blood drawn at Cottonwood County Hospital today," Shelby said. "I'll ask for the results to be forwarded to all parties."

Finally, after another clipped speech about how sorry the administrator was and that she'd call the moment the DNA test results reached her desk, the attorneys left, and Shelby and Liam Mercer were alone.

Liam had the same expression on his face that Shelby had to have on hers. Shock. Confusion. And fear. He was looking down but not at his son or at the floor.

"I'm hanging on to useless hope," she said. "If Shane isn't my biological son, if the babies were switched, then the baby in your arms is my child?" She shook her head. "This is crazy."

"Alexander is my son," Liam practically growled, his expression so fierce she took a step back. "Sorry," he said. "I know you're going through the same thing I am. I don't mean to take this out on you, of all people."

She bit her lip and let out a breath. Was the baby in Liam's arms her son? Had she walked out of this clinic six months ago with someone else's child? And left her own behind? Tears pricked her eyes.

"May I see him?" Shelby asked, blinking back hard on the tears. "Up close?"

Liam hesitated, then stepped toward her. Shelby tried to stifle the gasp. Alexander Mercer did look an awful lot like her. Down to the shape of the eyes, his face, something in his expression and the little Ingalls birthmark. But he had a dimple—like Liam. None of the Ingallses had a dimple.

But Shane's father did.

Still, hair and eye color and a birthmark and a dimple didn't mean Shane wasn't her son.

Even if the baby in her arms looked a lot like Liam Mercer.

Shelby shook her head, suddenly unable to speak. She sucked in a breath. "I love Shane with all my heart. I'm his only parent. I'm his mother. He's my son."

"I feel the same way about Alexander," Liam said. "His mother died in childbirth."

Oh, no. That was why he looked the way he had that night. "I'm so sorry." She let out a breath. "And I'm scared. Really, really scared."

"I don't say this often, Ms. Ingalls. But so am I."

That made her feel better. Especially because he was a Mercer. And the Mercer name in Wedlock Creek meant two things. Power and money. Shelby barely broke even every month. And her lawyer was on loan.

"Liam," she said. "My son looks a lot like you. And your son looks a lot like me."

He turned away, then stared down at the baby in his arms. Then at her. Then back to his son. "Yeah.

I know. And I'm worried as hell. That the babies actually could have been switched. I mean, I saw you here, in this clinic, in labor, at the same time Alexander's mother was in labor. I saw you with my own eyes. You gave birth to a baby boy. That's not in dispute. If Shane isn't yours, then…" He shook his head, then stared at the ground.

She expelled a breath. "So now what?"

Alexander gurgled and cooed, "Du, wa," his gaze on Shane. The two babies eyed each other, smiles forming. Alexander reached out to touch Shane's arm and Shane smiled, reaching to touch the brim of the little Stetson.

"They like each other," Liam said softly, his voice hollow. "Look, let's go to the hospital and get your and Shane's blood drawn for typing. For all we know, the clinic here has been making mistakes for years. Let's find out for sure that you and Shane *can't* be related."

Should she go anywhere with Liam Mercer? Maybe she should run it by her lawyer. But then again, there was only one person on earth who knew what this insanity felt like: Liam. She wanted to hear what he had to say. She needed to be around him right now.

She let out a breath and nodded. "I'm in no position to drive. My hands will shake on the wheel."

"I'll drive. I'll install Shane's seat in the back of my SUV."

Which meant he was calm. Outwardly, anyway. Because he knew that no matter what, he wouldn't lose anything? That was very likely how things were for Mercers. Money and power talked.

"I want to make something clear, Mr. Mercer. I know the Mercer name. You and your family are wealthy and powerful and own half the commercial real estate and the rodeo. I'm a single mother without much to my name but a secondhand shop. Regardless, if you push me, if you try anything underhanded, I'll fight you with everything I have."

"Whoa," he said, his blue eyes steady on her. "We're going through the same thing, Ms. Ingalls. We're in the same position. Money and power are meaningless here. If Alexander isn't my biological son, all the money in Wyoming won't make it any less true."

She stared at him. He was right—to a point. Money and power *could* take Shane away from her. He could end up with *both* boys.

"I might be rich, Ms. Ingalls. But I'm not underhanded. I'm a single parent, just like you are. And I'll swear on anything you want. I'll never do anything to hurt you or these babies."

The sincerity on his face made her feel better. And truth be told, she needed to believe him or she'd spontaneously combust. "Call me Shelby."

He nodded. "And call me Liam."

He gestured for her to walk ahead out the door. "Let's get the hell out of this clinic."

As she watched Liam zip up his son's fleece bunting, the tenderness on the man's face almost stole her breath.

He loves that baby. Like I love Shane.

Dear God, this was a mess.

You're my son, no matter what, she whispered silently to Shane.

As they left the office, each holding a baby, Shelby was barely hanging on. If the DNA tests proved the impossible, that they'd each taken home a baby who wasn't theirs, *would* Liam try to seek custody of both babies and win because of his power and money and influence? Right now it was easy for him to say he'd never do anything to hurt her. His back wasn't up against a wall—yet, anyway. Not like hers was.

Stop getting ahead of yourself, Shelby. He might be a Mercer, but she had a loud, bossy, big family in Wedlock Creek. They'd have her back. Her sister had managed to supply her with a lawyer in less than five minutes, after all. *One step at a time, one piece of information at a time.*

Feeling a little stronger, she watched as Liam headed across the parking lot to his car, a sleek, black SUV, settled Alexander in his car seat, then drove it over to where she stood next to her twelve-year-old Ford.

She could not, would not, lose Shane. But the little boy in that black car was very likely her baby, too.

Oh, God. Suddenly she wanted to tear Alexander from his car seat, take him in her arms and explain it had been a mistake, she hadn't known, she was so sorry she let someone else take him home and raise him these past six months.

As tears slipped down her cheeks, she felt a hand on her shoulder.

She hadn't even realized Liam had gotten out of his car and had come over to her. "We'll figure this out together," he said.

At the word *together*, she calmed down again and looked up into Liam Mercer's eyes. She saw sincerity there. But the last time Shelby had trusted a man she'd ended up pregnant and alone.

Careful, she told herself. Proceed with utmost caution. *Agree to nothing. Sign nothing. You're a smart woman. Keep your head.*

She was glad when Liam let go of her shoulder and opened her car door to get Shane's car seat, busy with installing it in his SUV. They were not united. They were not anything. His use of the word *together* would likely only serve him. She didn't know this man at all.

She was on her own here and had to remember that. Or she'd lose everything.

Liam's hands had been steady on the wheel during the drive to the hospital, but inside he was a mess. Every time his mind latched on something that would make Alexander his biological son, three more *yeah, but what about xyz, yeah, but remember when the administrator said* socked him upside the head. Shelby had been silent for the almost hour drive, and he was glad. He didn't want to talk about any of it. He could barely handle thinking about it.

Alexander wasn't his son? He damned well was, no matter what a piece of paper said. That was the one thing that kept reverberating in his head. He was sure it was the same for Shelby, which made him want to be around her and never see her again at the same time.

Was the baby in the back seat, the one without the cowboy hat, his biological child?

Maybe. Probably? No. Yes. He went round and round as Shelby and Shane were ushered into the lab room to get their blood drawn. As he sat in the waiting room, Alexander playing his favorite game of squeeze Daddy's chin, women around him commenting on Alexander's cuteness and big cheeks, he could hear Shane crying behind the closed door. Which made him hyperaware of the timing; his tiny vein had just been pricked, a vial filling with his blood. Which would prove, once and for all, if the clinic hadn't made a mistake with the typing. From prior visits, at that.

Hell, it was unlikely, but he was hanging on to hope. If Shelby *could* be Shane's biological mother, then they could all just walk away, go back to their lives and live happily-ever-after. Liam would have one heck of a story for tonight's dinner at the Mercer ranch.

Shelby finally came out of the lab room, holding Shane, who had a little round Mickey Mouse Band-Aid in the crook of his right arm. Liam stared at his little tear-stained face, seeing not only his own expression in Shane's, but Liza's, also.

He almost fell out of his chair.

"Are you all right, Liam?" Shelby asked, rushing over.

He slowly shook his head. He was not all right.

Calm down and go back to hanging on to hope. Wait for the blood results. If they still say Shelby isn't Shane's mother, then you'll wait for the DNA tests. You're Alexander's father. You are.

As they left the hospital, Shelby told him that the lab had promised to expedite the results, based on a call from the clinic requesting it. She would know by three o'clock today.

"I want to stay with you and Shane until we know," he said. "I need you in my sight."

"Because you're afraid I'll run away with your heir?" she snapped. "If Shane is your son, then Alexander is *my* son," she reminded him, her green eyes flashing.

He stared at her. "You really don't trust me, do you?"

"I don't know you," she pointed out. "And I don't trust easily. Add in who you are…"

"I told you, Shelby, I—"

"Won't do anything to hurt me or Shane. I know. I've tucked that away to remind you of it when you really have to face the truth of what's happened."

He shook his head. "Let me change how I put it, then. I want you and Shane in my sight because I'm going out of my mind. I don't want to be alone, but I don't want to tell anyone about this yet. That leaves you. To be with someone who gets it without my having to say a word."

Her expression softened. "I know exactly what you mean." She glanced at her watch. "Oh, God, I really need to head over to my shop and put a sign on the door that we're closed for the day. The Minnow sisters are probably worried about me, and I had an appointment scheduled for ten-thirty to look through a bag of stuff."

"Minnow sisters? Bag of stuff?"

"For Treasures, my shop. The Minnows are three elderly sisters who stop by every Friday at ten to see what I've added for the weekend shoppers."

He nodded. "The secondhand store. Next to the bakery, right? My cousin Clara loves that place. I once complimented a painting of a weathered red barn in her hallway and she said she got it from Treasures. I stopped by one day to check it out but left when I realized it was a secondhand store."

She raised an eyebrow. "Why doesn't that surprise me? Honestly, you never know what you'll find at Treasures."

Like dust? Falling apart old junk even its owner
didn't want? The painting had to be an exception.
"Well, why don't we head over there? We can talk
there or not talk there and just keep each other occu-
pied until the call comes from the hospital lab. I could
use a few cups of coffee. At some point later I'll drive
you back to the clinic to pick up your car."

Forty-five minutes later Liam pulled into a spot in
front of Treasures. As they got out of the car, Shelby
taking out Shane, and Liam taking out Alexander,
he saw Shelby craning her neck to look down Main
Street.

"I can just make out the Minnow sisters heading
into the library," she said. "They're easy to spot since
they always walk three across the sidewalk. They must
have waited all this time for me and gave up."

As she opened the door with an ornate gold key, he
realized he actually had been in the shop once before
with Clara. His cousin had insisted on dragging him
along to find a present for her mother, who despite
being Liam's dear aunt, was the biggest snob alive.
Liam hadn't thought his aunt would want anything
from a secondhand shop, but the next time he'd seen
her, she'd been wearing the brooch that Clara had insisted she'd love. *It's antique, it's history, it has a story*,
Clara had insisted. *Who knows where the brooch has
been, what love story it was part of. It's so romantic!*

It's so…*used*, was what Liam had thought. He appreciated the shiny and new. But hey, if it worked for
his cousin and aunt, all the better for Shelby, now that
he actually knew the shop's owner.

"I'll keep the shade drawn on the door and the
closed sign hanging," she said as they stepped inside.

"I hate to disappoint my customers or keep new ones away, but I can't open the store. Not in my frame of mind."

"I know what you mean," he said, scooting Alexander a bit higher in his arms. The baby snuggled against his leather jacket. "I had a day full of meetings, including a very important one. I canceled everything and delegated what I could." His cousin had been incredulous when he let her know he was counting on her to seal the deal on the Kenyon Corp acquisition, that he had full faith in her. Incredulous that he was skipping the meeting and that he believed in her so much; that part of their relationship had never really been tested before.

"What the hell could be so important that you'd miss the negotiation?" Clara had asked when he'd called her after dropping off Shelby and Shane at the hospital entrance. He'd let Shelby know he'd park and meet her after alerting his office he'd be out for the day.

"I can't talk about it right now, Clara. Just knock them dead."

"Oh, I will. Hope everything's okay."

"Talk to you in a few hours," he'd said and ended the call, which he knew would worry her, but his very focused cousin would set her mind to the negotiating and nothing else and she'd do great. She'd burn up his phone later and ring his doorbell until he answered later, though. Of that he had no doubt. To both tell him about the meeting and to hear what had kept him from it. But he had no idea when he'd be ready to talk about what was going on. *If* he'd talk about it.

He turned his attention to the stuffed shop, every

table, every bit of space, taken up by things, from lamps to flower pots and vases to cases of jewelry to paintings and knickknacks of every kind imaginable. There was a bookcase of old, leather-bound classics and an entire table full of various teapots with little cups and saucers.

He glanced up at the wall near the shop's entrance. "Look, Alexander, it's a cuckoo clock. The little bird is about to come out because it's almost the half hour." He walked a bit closer and as the clock chimed that it was 1:30 p.m., a gold bird with a red beak popped out.

Alexander giggled and pointed.

"Cuckoo," Liam said. "Cuckoo!" Yup, this whole thing was *cuckoo*, all right.

Alexander giggled, and Liam smiled, snuggling his little boy close.

She smiled. "Fatherhood agrees with you."

He looked at Alexander, the little boy he loved more than anything on earth. "Alexander changed my life. For the good."

"Must have been hard, though, going from Wedlock Creek's most prized eligible bachelor to the father of an infant. On your own."

"It was. I guess I was too shocked to pay attention to how hard it was and just went day by day. But every night, when I'd be up with Alexander at two and four a.m., the house dead quiet except for his tiny burp after having his bottle, I was just overtaken by devotion. By a sense of responsibility to this little life I helped create."

She bit her lip and looked at him, then set Shane down in a bouncy seat behind the counter and handed him a teething ring in the shape of a rabbit. "With this...new information, I hate to put him down, for him to be out of arm's reach for even a moment, but honestly, he's getting big. He's eighteen pounds now."

Liam smiled. "So's Alexander." He glanced at Shane, watching the little stuffed animals twirl around on the mobile attached to the bouncer. "This is some mess, huh? Everything we thought we know about our lives is suddenly turned upside down."

She was staring at Shane, and he could see tears glistening in her eyes. He wanted to hold her, to tell her they'd get through this, somehow, that they'd get through it together. But what comfort would that be? They were practically strangers.

The light shining through the windows caught on her blond hair and the side of her delicate face, and she looked so alone and lost that he reached out and took her hand and gave it a gentle squeeze. *I'm not the enemy*, the squeeze was supposed to say. *But yeah, this sucks.*

She looked up at him, surprise crossing her pretty face, and she squeezed back.

"I have another bouncer if you want a breather yourself," she said.

"Sure."

She disappeared into a back room and returned with a yellow bouncer with a stars and moon mobile. Alexander pointed at it.

"You like it?" Liam asked the baby. "Let's get you settled in it next to your buddy, Shane."

He put Alexander in the bouncer, buckling the little harness, and turned the reclining seat so that the boys could see each other. He stood and came back around the counter when Shelby's phone rang.

She glanced at the cuckoo clock. "It's only one forty-five. Could that be the hospital lab?" Her phone rang again, but she seemed frozen in place. On the third ring she grabbed it from her tote bag. "Shelby Ingalls speaking."

"It's them," she mouthed to him, the phone against her ear. He watched her listen, her eyes full of hope. *Tell me what I want to hear*, those eyes beseeched. But then the light went out of the green depths, and she clearly couldn't contain the sob that rose from inside her.

She croaked out a "Thank you for calling," then put the phone down on a table next to a teapot, her eyes welling, anguish dropping her to her knees on the circular rug.

"Oh, no," he said, closing his eyes for a moment. Oh, no. No.

She burst into tears. "It's official. Shane is not my son."

Chapter Three

Liam rushed over and knelt down beside her. He put his arm around her. "I'm so sorry, Shelby."

"It has to be true, then," she said. "The hospital switched the babies. How else could this have happened?"

Intellectually, he was beginning to believe it. In his heart, though, Alexander West Mercer was his son. Plain and simple.

Except it was no longer so plain or simple.

"The baby right there," she said, staring at Alexander in his bouncy seat, smiling up at the colorful mobile dangling above. "He's my son? That's what the DNA tests will reveal. I took home the wrong baby. How could I not know my own child? How?"

He felt his cells, his blood, the air in the lungs, come to a dead stop. *My son. My son. My son.* He wanted her to stop saying those words. Alexander was *his* son.

But he was going to have to accept the truth. Two baby boys had been born early in the morning of November 5. One couldn't be Shelby's child. Which meant the other was.

"They do look alike," he said. "And given the chaos in those moments after they were born, you probably barely got to hold him, let alone study his face in the dark."

She bit her lip, squeezing her eyes shut.

"We both took home the wrong baby," he added, his gaze on Shane in his own bouncy seat, biting the little teething ring. When he looked at Shane Ingalls, he saw a beautiful baby boy, someone else's beautiful baby boy. He felt no connection. What did that mean?

"I want to talk to the nurse who switched them," Liam said. "I need to hear what happened. Of course I know she can't be certain, that it's only what makes sense, given the blood type issue and the delay in putting identification bracelets on the babies, but I need to hear her tell me herself."

Shelby wiped under her eyes and tilted her head. "*Can* we talk to her?"

"We can do whatever the hell we want. She's no longer employed by the clinic. The director said she retired three months ago."

Shelby nodded. "I'd like to hear it from her about what happened, too."

"I'll call Anne Parcells and ask for the contact information. She may be cagey about it. Anne has to be worried about a lawsuit. The nurse, as well."

"*Are* you thinking about a lawsuit?" she asked.

"Well, first we need back the DNA tests that con- clusively prove we took home the wrong babies. But if the nurse made an honest mistake in the chaos of a blizzard that knocked out power..."

Shelby nodded. "An honest mistake is an honest mistake even if it's turned our lives around. And who knows what this will mean for Shane and Alexander."

"Meaning?"

She shrugged. "Well, what's going to happen now? What's going to happen when the DNA test says I have your son and you have mine?"

He sucked in a breath.

"I want to hold Alexander but I'm afraid to," she said, wrapping her arms around herself as if protec- tively.

He stiffened, everything inside him going numb. "I know. Because if you hold him, knowing what you know, you're afraid you won't be able to hand him back over. It's why I haven't asked to hold Shane." He'd have to face the truth, then, that Shane was his, that he'd left him behind, and he wasn't sure he could handle that.

She stared at Alexander, who was smiling at the mobile and then looking at his little buddy, biting on his teething toy. "He has my eyes and the Ingalls straight and pointy nose. We all have that nose."

"It's a good one," he said. Liam's nose was more Roman. And Liza's had been long.

"My head is going to explode," she said. "I can't think. I can barely stand up anymore."

"I know. Same here."

"I think I need to just go upstairs to my apartment, with Shane, and just let this all sink in."

He nodded. "I think that's a good idea. I could use some time alone to try to process this, too." He headed over to where Alexander sat in the bouncer.

"Liam, I'm very close to my family, particularly my sister. I don't think I can keep this from them until the DNA tests are in. Especially because I have no doubt anymore that the babies were switched. And to be honest, I don't want to keep it from them. I need their support."

He nodded again, letting his head drop back a little. "I can understand that. I'm not all that close to my parents or my brother, but I wish I were. I'm close to my cousin Clara, the one who likes your shop."

An idea started forming and he dismissed it. Then came back to it. It involved inviting Shelby to the family dinner tonight. Shelby and Shane. He could drop the bombshell and they'd all have a chance to meet the Ingallses. It would be a way to get the conversation over with.

"Maybe getting our families' takes on the situation is a good idea," he said. "The Mercers get together every Friday night for dinner, a tradition going back generations. Why don't you join us? You and Shane. We can tell them together."

"I thought you said your weren't close with your family. Weekly family dinners—on a weekend night, no less. That sounds close."

"I think we all keep doing it because we want something to change but it never does, and the weekly dinners make us feel like we're doing something to change it. But the evening always ends in arguments or stony silences, mostly because my brother won't go into the family business, which is nothing new. He's a cowboy on a cattle ranch."

"Well, he'll sure be glad to see me and Shane, then," she said. "Talk about taking the focus off him."

Liam laughed, and for a moment he was surprised he had any laughter in him. "I think he'll be thrilled. He may actually hug me."

"How do you think your parents will take the news?" she asked.

"Like we did. Who the hell can process this?"

She smiled, lighting up her pretty face. "Right?"

He smiled back. Then felt it fade. "But no matter what, Shelby, *we* decide what will happen. You and me. No matter how forceful or strong our families come on about this. I decide nothing without you, and you decide nothing without me. Deal?"

She stared at him hard for a moment. "Deal."

He picked up Alexander from the bouncer seat, darting a glance at Shane. At the baby he had to accept was his flesh and blood. But it didn't feel real or even possible. His head and heart were not computing, as was often the case.

"Pick you up at six-thirty?" he asked. "Cocktails at six forty-five, dinner at seven."

"I'd prefer to meet you there," she said. "I think. Yes, I'll meet you."

He nodded. "I'll drive you over to the clinic so you can get your car," he said, hoisting up Alexander and heading toward the door.

He felt numb as she scooped up Shane and followed him. They were both quiet on the ride to the clinic. He watched her open up the back door of her car and buckle in Shane. As she went around to the driver's side, she held up a hand as if saying goodbye. For now, anyway.

He held up a hand too, then started his car. Part of him was relieved to be on his own with his son, his beloved Alexander. *We're safe*, he thought the moment he pulled out of the lot.

But left behind, again, was his biological child.

Someone was ringing both doorbells—to the shop and the upstairs apartment—like a lunatic, pressing it so many times and holding it that Shelby's poor cat, Luna, darted under her favorite velvet chair.

"I'm coming, I'm coming," she called, turning around on the back stairs. She'd been on the way up to her apartment, Shane in one arm and her overstuffed tote in the other. Liam had just left five minutes ago. Could he be back? She hurried down the stairs and peered through the filmy curtain at the window.

Twenty-six-year-old Norah Ingalls, in her uniform of black pants, a white T-shirt and yellow apron with Pie Diner in sparkly blue letters across, looked frantic, her strawberry-blond hair pulled back in a messy ponytail. Shelby let her in.

"You haven't returned my texts!" Norah said, hands on hips. "Or my calls. The shop is closed at three in the afternoon. Four people at the diner mentioned it's been closed *all day*. What the hell, Shelby? What is going on? David wouldn't tell me a thing. Which freaked me out even more."

Shelby closed the door behind her sister. "Let's go upstairs. I need to be home for this, to actually say the words to another person for the first time."

Norah's hazel eyes widened. "Jesus, you're scaring me, Shel."

"It's a doozy," Shelby said, leading the way up the stairs to the apartment.

The moment Shelby unlocked the door at the top of the stairs she felt better. Home. She'd lived here for the past five years, ever since she'd opened Treasures with a little help from an unexpected small inheritance the Ingalls sisters received from their late grandmother. The apartment was like the store—old but with some beautiful architectural details, arched doorways and big windows that let in great light. She'd decorated the place with finds from estate sales, where she bought most of her goods for the shop. Whenever she was up here she felt at peace. And she needed that feeling to tell her sister what was going on.

"Let me put Shane down for his nap and I'll be right back, Norah."

The hands were back on Norah's hips. "I can't take another second, Shelby Rae Ingalls. Tell me now!"

"Two seconds, I promise. Shane is zonked. He'll go right out."

She slipped into the nursery, painted soothing shades of pale yellow and blue, cradling Shane against her before putting him in the crib. He let out a cry, then a sigh, his blue eyes drooping. He fussed for a few moments, but Shelby sang his favorite song, about the itsy bitsy spider, and his eyes drooped even more.

She watched him for a moment, closing her own eyes, bracing herself against the truth and for having to actually talk about what had happened today. Norah would be the first person she'd tell.

She closed the nursery door and headed back into

the living room, where Norah was holding two bottles of whiskey that a handyman had given Shelby a couple weeks ago for taking so long to fix the washing machine.

"I'm gonna need this, right?" Norah asked. "Both bottles, from the expression on your face."

"Yes," Shelby said, and this time her sister's eyes went even wider. She attempted something of a smile, took the whiskey bottles back into the kitchen and poured two glasses of white wine instead. Norah followed her in, standing in the doorway. "Okay. Here goes," she said, handing her sister a glass.

Norah gulped half the glass of wine. "I'm ready. Whatever it is, whatever you need, I'm here for you."

Tears streamed down Shelby's face. She stood there in her kitchen and bawled.

Norah burst into tears, too. "Oh, God. Oh, God. You're sick."

Shelby froze. She wasn't sick. No one was dying. *Get ahold of yourself, Shelby.* Perspective. With that, she launched into the whole story, starting with the meeting at the clinic, explaining about having her blood retested at the hospital and ending with being invited to Liam Mercer's family ranch for dinner tonight.

Norah's open mouth and chin kept dropping lower. She stared at Shelby with *what the?* shock on her face, then raced over and enveloped Shelby in a long hug, both of them sobbing. Her sister wiped under her eyes and gave Shelby's hand a squeeze before dropping down on a chair at the round table in front of the window. "I seriously think my legs are going to give out. I just can't believe this." She opened her mouth as if

to ask a question, then clamped it shut. Then again.
Then again. "It's not sinking in, Shelby."

Shelby sat down across from Norah. "I know. I
don't even think I've processed it. It's just buzzing
around at the forefront of my mind like a bee that
won't go away."

"What's Liam Mercer like? I've seen him around.
He's hard to miss."

Shelby took a sip of wine. "I know. Gorgeous.
Amazing body. And surprisingly nice."

A strawberry-blond eyebrow shot up. "Really? He
didn't threaten you?"

"About taking Shane? No. I don't think it's sunk
in for him at all that Shane is his child. Or he's not
ready to believe it. I think he'll need the results of the
DNA test for that. His blood type is compatible with
Alexander's, as is the baby's mother's. As is mine. So
I guess he's still holding out hope that his life can go
back to exactly what it was seven hours ago."

Norah shook her head. "If he does threaten you,
we'll sic David on him."

Shelby reached across the table and squeezed her
sister's hand, glad she'd rung the bell like a lunatic,
after all. "It's good to be dating a lawyer. I'll tell everyone else tomorrow morning. I need to just lie down
and breathe before getting ready for dinner at the Mercers'."

"God, have you seen that place?" Norah asked. "I
didn't know ranches could have mansions on them."

She thought back to what Liam had said, that all
the money and power in Wyoming couldn't make the
truth any less true.

She wasn't sure if that helped or not.

* * *

As Liam watched his brother hoist Alexander high in the air in the family room, as close to baby talk with an "up you go!" as Drake Mercer got, he found himself studying Drake's face and hair and the dimple that deepened when he laughed every time Alexander giggled. Liam had been studying his family since he'd arrived ten minutes ago for the weekly Mercer family dinner. Last Friday night his mother had remarked over the Italian wedding soup course how Alexander was looking more and more like his handsome grandfather every day, especially around the eyes and "something in the expression." He wondered now if coloring was enough to make people see similarities where otherwise there was none—when people knew they were related.

He'd always figured Alexander must look more like Liza's side of the family, though he'd never really seen Liza in Alexander's face. And since Liza had been raised by a few different foster families, she'd never known her family.

"I knew you were going to be a rancher like me," Drake said, tapping the tiny Stetson Harrington Mercer had bought for Alexander.

"A *weekend* cowboy, like me," Harrington corrected. "That's how it's done. You devote your weekdays to the family business and the weekends to appreciating the land. Every Mercer has done it that way for generations."

"A real cowboy, weekend or otherwise, walks his own way, blazes his own path," Drake said, hoisting up Alexander again and earning a giggle.

"A real man puts family first, Drake," Harrington said, his tone its usual imperious don't-bother-arguing.

Drake didn't bother. He'd long stopped. He'd say his piece to a point, but he knew he was talking to a brick wall.

Liam admired his brother. He'd been blazing that own path since he was knee-high, doing things his way, taking the punishment and lecture rather than follow rules that didn't make sense to him or came from someone else's rigid vision for how he should act and think. Now, at twenty-seven, Drake was the foreman's right-hand man on a very prosperous cattle ranch and would likely take over the retiring-age man's job in the next year or two.

Liam had never thought he and his brother looked that much alike, but as he studied Drake, he could see how similar their features were. They had their mom's blue eyes and thick, dark hair, though Drake wore his a bit longer and messier than Liam did. Liam had his mother's strong, straight nose, while Drake more resembled Harrington Mercer.

How could someone who looks so much like me be so different from me in every way? their father would mutter at many a family dinner.

He glanced at his son, whom Uncle Drake was now setting down in the giant playpen by the sliding glass doors to the deck. Now that he knew that Alexander was very likely Shelby's son, he saw Shelby in his sweet little face.

"Must we have the same conversation every Friday?" Larissa Mercer asked, dusting her hands on her apron as she emerged from the kitchen, the smell of something delicious wafting out. His mother loved to cook and was working her way through one of the Barefoot Contessa's Italian cookbooks. "We're here together. That's what matters. Let's just enjoy ourselves."

Harrington Mercer gave Drake a half frown and poured himself a drink. Before he could respond, the doorbell rang.

Shelby. And Shane.

"I should have mentioned this earlier—I invited a friend to dinner," Liam announced. "She also has a six-month-old." He'd had a few hours to let his mother know. He also could have mentioned it when he'd arrived. But he'd found himself unable to get the words out.

Plus, he'd be hit with a barrage of questions about who Shelby was to him—with the assumption that they were a couple. Liam hadn't brought a woman to a family dinner in a couple of years, since he'd gotten his heart stomped on as a love-struck twenty-three-year-old bursting with a marriage proposal. Then two years ago he'd finally gotten serious again with another woman, a VP at Mercer Industries whom he'd discovered had been more interested in him as a stepping stone and left MI high and dry in the middle of a merger when she'd gotten a better offer from a rival company. Then a year ago there was Liza, whom he might have fallen for if he hadn't been so guarded against betrayal. But Liza had always said she had no interest in meeting his snooty, highfalutin family, which had made him laugh. All she'd wanted from Liam was his time and attention, and he hadn't even been willing to give that. She'd been right to dump him when he told her he wasn't interested in marriage or children—probably ever.

His mother's eyes lit up. "Ah, a new love interest!" She turned toward the family room, where her husband and younger son were ignoring each other in opposite corners. "Ooh, Harrington, did you hear? Liam's bringing home a girlfriend to meet us!" She turned back to Liam. "I had a feeling you'd fall for a single mother of a baby. Gives you quite a bit in common from the start."

Liam headed toward the door. "Actually, Shelby is just a friend."

His mother smiled slyly. "Sure she is. You've never invited a *friend* to Friday dinner before."

Liam pulled open the door, and the sight of Shelby stopped him cold. It wasn't just that she was beautiful; she was. But she suddenly seemed so…necessary, as if he couldn't get through the day without being with her and had just realized it when he saw her face.

That was nuts.

They were in the middle of one hell of a thing. That was it. She was like a lifeline. She was the other half in this. Not his other half, of course, but the other half in this insanity. It made sense that he needed her to feel some sense of grounding.

"It's good to see you," he said very honestly. "Hey there, Shane. You look very handsome in your lasso-print onesie." Sometimes he still couldn't get over that the word *onesie* was a big part of his vocabulary.

She laughed, setting him more at ease, and he was struck by her green eyes. He saw so much in those eyes. Worry. Confusion. Anxiety. But if he wasn't mistaken, she was also glad to see him.

She peered behind him, and he turned to find his entire family standing in front in the arched doorway to the family room, clearly eager to get a glimpse of the woman who'd gotten herself invited to the Mercer family dinner.

"Everyone, meet Shelby Ingalls and her son, Shane. Shelby, this is my mother, my father and my brother, Drake."

Everyone smiled and started talking about how cute Shane was. Everyone except Liam's father. In fact, Harrington Mercer was glaring at Shane. Really. His dad was glaring at a baby. What the hell was his problem?

"A word, Liam," his dad said, his tone cold, his expression...angry.

He glanced at Shelby standing next to his mother, oblivious to anything but Shane, whom she'd asked to hold. "Just going to talk to my dad for a second. Be right back."

Shelby nodded, and he followed his father to the library.

Harrington Mercer closed the door, then pointed his finger at Liam's chest. "Now you listen to me, Liam. I overlooked one illegitimate kid because of the circumstances and you're raising him. But if you think this other one is going to have the same privileges as Alexander, you're wrong."

Liam stared at his father, no idea what the hell he was going on about. *"What?"*

"Clearly, Shelby's child is yours. He looks exactly like you. And considering the babies are the same age, I'll say it now, Liam—use condoms for God's sake."

Liam might have laughed at how ludicrous this conversation was, but nothing about it was funny. "I have an announcement to make, Dad. I want to say it once and to everyone. So let's head back."

Harrington frowned. "Trust me, you don't have to announce anything. It's obvious just from looking at the baby." His father shook his head but followed Liam.

He stood beside Shelby, so close he could smell her shampoo. "Ready?" he whispered to her.

"Not really," she said. "But I'll never be."

"I have an announcement," he called out, and his brother glanced at him, then lifted his dark eyebrows at the seriousness of Liam's expression.

"What is it, dear?" his mother asked, coming closer and wrapping her arm around her husband's.

He cleared his throat, took one last look at Shelby, then said, "This morning, the Wedlock Creek Clinic called and asked me to bring in Alexander—and my attorney. Shelby got the same call." He looked at Shelby, so beautiful in her blue dress, her blond hair loose around her shoulders. He told them everything, from what the director had said to the DNA testing to Shelby getting the call to confirm that she couldn't be her baby's mother.

"We should get the DNA results in about a week," Shelby said, her voice a bit tight and strange-sounding.

"So now I have two nephews," Drake said. "That's kind of awesome."

Liam smiled at his brother. His younger sibling had a way of always defusing a situation.

"This is very sudden," Harrington said, frowning. "Of course, until the DNA results are in, there's no reason to assume that the babies were switched. Alexander is our grandchild, same as always, and Shelby's child is hers."

"But Shelby's child *can't* be hers biologically, Dad," Liam said. "Which means the two male babies born the night of November 5 were switched."

Harrington lifted his chin. "If that is truly the case, I'll call my own lawyer about getting the lawsuit going. That inept clinic needs to be shut down."

"No," Shelby said. "The clinic serves the entire county. It takes the poorest residents who don't have insurance. What happened was an honest mistake during the blizzard back in November when the power went out and the clinic's generators failed twice."

Harrington stared at her. "Well, the generators shouldn't have failed. The backup is supposed to *back up.*"

"First of all, Dad, I don't have conclusive proof that Alexander isn't my biological son. I won't know for certain until the DNA tests."

"Proof that he *isn't?*" Harrington snapped. "You sound like you believe this nonsense."

Ha. A minute ago his father was *sure* Shane was Liam's child. "I'm facing facts."

His father stared at Alexander in his playpen, still wearing his little brown cowboy hat, then slid a glance at Shane in Shelby's arms. "So this," he said, pointing at Shane, "is my true grandchild?"

What the hell, Liam thought. *True* grandchild? "Alexander is your true grandchild, regardless, Dad," Liam and his brother said at practically the same time.

"This is quite a mess." Larissa Mercer patted at her ash-blond hair. "I say we sit down to dinner and talk about something more pleasant. As your father said, until the DNA results come in, there's no need to discuss it."

"We should prepare for the truth to come," Shelby said softly.

Liam glanced at her and had the urge to hold her hand, in solidarity, in needing her strength, in offering her his. "I agree."

"Do you like salmon, Shelby?" Larissa asked. "I've made a heavenly balsamic-glazed grilled salmon with new potatoes."

Liam looked at Shelby, his expression hopefully telling her that his mother just couldn't handle this right now. They would talk salmon instead.

"I love salmon," Shelby said with a gentle smile. She looked around the room. "I love your house, Mrs. Mercer."

Relief crossed Larissa Mercer's face, and she linked arms with Shelby. "Come, dear, you can test-taste a potato and tell me if it's ready."

As the women left the room, Liam watched his father walk across the floor and pretend great interest in rearranging the glasses on the bar.

"You okay?" Drake asked, taking Alexander from the playpen and holding him.

Liam stared at his son. His son. "Not really."

"This may get seriously complicated," Drake said. "You know that."

Liam frowned. "Shelby's a good person. I have no doubt of that and I barely know her."

"I'm not referring to Shelby," Drake said, his gaze moving to Harrington Mercer.

Liam felt a quick, hot poke at his gut. "Well, we'll

find out what a real cowboy truly is, then, won't we?"
he said.

Not even sure himself what he meant.

Chapter Four

Dinner had been an awkward nightmare. Shelby had never been so happy to leave anywhere in her entire life. Of course, she didn't know Liam Mercer very well, but even a total stranger could see the man was tense.

"Oh, Shelby, wait!" Larissa Mercer said as they stood in the doorway, about to make their escape. "I have something for your shop."

Shelby turned around and smiled, surprised. That was unexpected. Larissa opened the foyer closet and amid some coats and rain boots, Shelby could see a large plastic container marked *Donate*. She pulled out a medium-size plain brown bag with little handles and handed it to Shelby. "Here you go. Someone left it on the porch a few weeks ago and I've been meaning to bring it over to Treasures. It's one of those musical jewelry boxes. It works, too—plays one of my favorite Mozart piano sonatas."

Shelby glanced in the bag, but the box was wrapped in newspaper. "That's very kind of you to donate it to Treasures. I wonder why someone left it on your porch."

Larissa shrugged. "Harrington's name is on the bag," she said, pointing to the black script across the front. "Your father shrugged when I asked him about it. I guess someone left it as a thank-you for something or other. But there's not a drop of space for another thing in this house, so you take it, Shelby. It's lovely and someone will indeed 'treasure' it."

Liam reached over and hugged his mother, his shoulders relaxing. "Thanks for dinner, Mom."

"Ahlabawa," Alexander cooed, looking at his grandfather with his big blue eyes.

"Bye now," Harrington Mercer said, nodding at all of them and then turning away.

Larissa sighed and leaned forward. "It's a lot to take in. Let him digest it."

"It *is* a lot to take in," Shelby agreed. "Thanks again for the donation."

The moment the Mercers' stately red door closed behind Larissa, Shelby breathed a sigh of relief. Everyone—except for Drake—had eaten in record time and then made excuses for having to disappear. Dinner had taken all of fifteen minutes.

Liam half smiled in the illumination of the porch light. "Yeah, I know," he said in response to absolutely nothing. No words were needed.

She smiled. "Every Friday, huh? You're made of strong stuff."

They headed to their cars, Liam with a baby carrier in each hand, Shelby holding the bag Larissa had given her. Liam shrugged. "I don't know why I expect my father to be different, but I always do. I always wish he'll say: 'Whatever you need, Liam. I'm here for you.' My mom tries, but she's an ignorer, a rug sweeper-under." He shook his head. "I guess they have a right to their own take on things."

Shelby touched his arm, her heart going out to him. "Well, it had to be a shock for them. They're Alexander's grandparents. Their lives are turned upside down, too."

He frowned. "Pretending the situation doesn't exist and talking about gardening and the new gift shop on Main Street isn't going to make the situation any less crazy."

Truth be told, Shelby had appreciated the small talk about spring bulbs and how the gift shop sold a simply delightful rose-scented hand cream in the loveliest packaging. For the half hour she'd spent in the Mercer mansion, she'd almost forgotten the events of the day. Almost. Being forced to talk about something else, to think about something else, had been a good thing. "Your mom is right, though. Your dad just needs time to digest. To let it sink in."

He nodded and glanced down at Alexander in his baby carrier. "He's out cold."

"So's Shane," she said, reaching to caress a strand of silky brown hair in the breeze. "Liam, what are we supposed to do for a week until the results come in? Until we know for sure. How are we supposed to get through this? What are we supposed to *do*? I can't think straight."

"Me either. I could use a strong cup of coffee right now. That's all I know."

"I have a new bag of Sumatra beans," she said. "And really good chocolate cookies."

He smiled. "Your place, it is. I'll follow you."

Within a half hour they were on their second mugs of coffee and another cookie each in the eat-in kitchen in Shelby's apartment, both babies stirring in their carriers on the side table across from them. Shane began fussing, which made Alexander scowl and pipe up.

Shelby got up and was about to pick up Shane when she stopped and turned around.

"Liam?" She bit her lip, then rushed to get her thought out before she clamped down on it. "Maybe you should soothe Shane. And I'll pick up Alexander."

He put down his mug and stared at the boys in their carriers. Finally, he nodded and stood up, and she was suddenly so aware of his height and the breadth of him. Earlier he'd seemed like an adversary but now he felt more like an anchor somehow.

"You first," he said. "If that's okay."

She walked over to the table and kept her eyes on Alexander, trying not to let her gaze keep drifting to the little birthmark on his ear. Or how like her eyes his were.

"He can get a little fussy with newcomers," he said. "He likes his grandfather and uncle and two particular teachers at the day care. He's warming up to my cousin Clara and seems to save his spit-up for her."

He was being kind, she realized. Trying to let her know that if he squirmed and fussed in the arms of the woman who'd given birth to him, to not take it personally. She turned to him and smiled and he smiled back.

She undid the harness and scooped up the baby, cradling him against her. He slipped into her embrace as though he'd always known her, one little hand grabbing at her shirt, the other wrapping around a strand of her wavy blond hair. He looked up at her with those enormous blue eyes.

As tears pricked her own eyes, she turned away a bit, needing some privacy from Liam.

He seemed to get that. "I'll go pick up Shane now, if that's all right."

She whirled around, suddenly nervous despite this being her idea. "Okay."

She watched him walk over to the table and undo Shane's harness, then carefully pick him up and cuddle him against his chest.

"He feels like Alexander—like a six-month-old baby boy. But he's not Alexander."

"No," Shelby said. "He's not."

But as she looked down at the boy in her arms, the boy she knew was hers, too, all she could think was: *you're my flesh and blood. You're a part of me, a piece of me. But you're not mine.*

The tears threatened to spill over, and she blinked them back hard.

"He's been here in Wedlock Creek all these months and I had no idea," Liam said, his gaze on Shane, nestled in his arms. Shelby could see anger etched into his features, his jawline hard. "I've been denied my child and you've been denied yours."

And they both loved the babies they'd raised for the past six months, the babies they'd believed were their children. The babies who were their children. Shane was her son. Nothing, not a blood type, not DNA, not a court order, would change that.

"I see what you mean about not being able to give him back," Liam said. "I've missed out on six months."

"I know," she said, nuzzling her cheek against Alexander's head. "So what the hell do we do? What do we *do*?"

She couldn't leave Alexander, this precious bundle she held, this baby she'd brought into the world. She couldn't walk away, go home, open the shop, wait an endless week. She couldn't. She needed, wanted, to be around Alexander with the same fierce drive she needed to be around Shane.

"I don't want to put him down," Liam said, kissing Shane's head. "I don't want to give him back."

The tears did spill then. "I know. Me either. I don't want to leave him behind again."

"Exactly," Liam said, his gaze soft on Shane.

She felt Liam staring at her. When she looked up at him, she could see he was deciding something.

"Shelby, I have a proposition for you."

She tilted her head. "What kind of proposition?"

"Until the DNA tests come in," he said, "maybe we should think about the four of us being under one roof. Together."

"What? You're suggesting we live together? We don't even know each other!"

"Except you've been raising my son for the past six months and I've been raising yours. I want to know him, Shelby. I'm sure you want to know Alexander."

"Of course I do."

"I don't know how else to go about this. We've lost out on enough time."

"And if the results come back and the boys weren't switched?" she asked. "If the blood typing results were a mistake—even three times?"

"Then we can go back to our lives."

She stared at him. "And if the results come back and we know for sure the babies were switched at birth?"

"We'll cross that bridge if we get there, Shelby."

Live with Liam Mercer?

Live with Shane and Alexander. That was all she needed to know. "The kitchen floor slants a bit. And Drunk Pete likes to howl at the moon when he leaves the bar down the street every night. But the guest room bed is incredibly comfortable."

He raised an eyebrow. "I was thinking you'd move in with me. I live on a ranch on the outskirts of town. Well, it's not a working ranch, but I do have two horses. There's a lot of room and everything a six-month-old baby could want."

His turf? No way. She bit her lip. "I have everything a six-month-old baby *needs*. And three bedrooms. We can bunk the boys in Shane's nursery. I'd prefer to be here, Liam, for many reasons. Including the fact that people often stop by to see if I want to purchase their unwanted treasures for the store. They know to ring my apartment bell during off hours."

"You sure do make yourself available to look through someone's old stuff."

"You know the old saying. One's man's junk… But it's more than that, Liam. Sometimes people need to get rid of things to finally let go, to say goodbye to parts of their past. I get that."

"There are parts of my past I wish I could let go of

that easily." He glanced around the apartment, his gaze stopping on the beads dangling down from a doorway. "Then I'll be back with my bags in a couple hours."

The day had begun with learning she wasn't Shane's mother.

It was ending with Shane's father moving into her home.

She didn't even want to fathom what tomorrow might have in store for her.

Nine p.m. was closing time at her family's Pie Diner, which meant Shelby would find her sister, her mom and her aunt Cheyenne in the main part of the diner or the kitchen, cleaning up and taking pies for tomorrow morning from the oven and leaving them to cool. She hadn't had much of an appetite at dinner, but she would never turn down a slice of pie, particularly chocolate cream, and on Fridays there was always chocolate cream. The Pie Diner was truly just that: pies, scrumptious, homemade and sliced generously. Every day there were various quiches, pot pies, and six kinds of dessert pies, and very few leftovers.

She entered the diner just as Norah was turning over the open sign.

Norah rushed over for a hug, and Shelby was so done from the day she practically went limp in her sister's arms. Norah took Shane's carrier and set it down on the counter. "One slice of chocolate cream pie and a lemon seltzer coming up. You okay?"

She waited until the fortifying pie was in front of her before answering. "Liam is moving in. With Alexander. Neither of us can bear to be away from Shane and Alexander, so it just makes sense to be together."

Norah's mouth dropped open. "Moving in? Shelby, are you sure?"

"I just know that I held Alexander tonight for the first time and I couldn't give him back. I didn't want to give him back. And it was the same when Liam held Shane."

"Oh, Shelby. I can totally understand that."

She forked a piece of pie, her appetite for her favorite dessert barely there. "I can't think straight. I can't see straight. Up is down, right is left. I need him and Alexander around me. Liam's going through the same thing I am. I can be a mess without having to say a word. He instantly knows how I feel. It's a comfort."

Norah nodded. "Well, if he so much as talks about trying to gain custody of Shane, you call David, you hear?"

"No one is talking about custody—at least until the DNA test results come in. And then, who knows? I have no idea what's going to happen, Norah."

"What's this about custody?" Shelby's mother asked, coming through the swinging door of the kitchen, her blond hair in a short ponytail. "Ooh, there's my precious grandbaby," she said, beelining for Shane in his carrier on the counter. She smothered her grandson with kisses, then noticed Shelby's expression. "Hey, what's wrong?"

"I've got news, Mom. Can you grab Aunt Cheyenne?"

"Everything okay, Shel?" Arlena Ingalls asked, her hazel-green eyes worried.

She shook her head. "No."

"Oh, God." Her mother's eyes filled with tears.

"I'm not sick," Shelby assured her. "It's nothing like that. But something crazy has happened."

Her mother bit her lip and hurried into the kitchen, then came out with Aunt Cheyenne. The Ingalls women were strong stock and Shelby knew she could count on them—for support, for advice.

Norah squeezed Shelby's hand in commiseration, and as her mother and sister stood behind the counter, staring at Shelby, she launched into the whole story. Starting with the call from the Wedlock Creek Clinic's administrator and ending with Liam packing his bags to move in with Alexander.

And then after a barrage of questions she couldn't really answer, they hugged her one by one and sent her home with a quiche Lorraine, a chicken pot pie, and three kinds of dessert pie, her favorite chocolate cream, a cherry and Arlena Ingalls's famed Comfort Custard Pie.

"It's gonna be okay," her sister said at the door. "It will."

"Just be careful, Shel," her aunt Cheyenne said, tossing her long auburn braid off her shoulder. "You say this Liam Mercer seems kind and reasonable, but the DNA test results aren't in yet. When those results say that Shane is his biological son, all hell is gonna break loose."

"That'll make Alexander Mercer my biological son," she reminded them. "We're both in the same boat in very choppy, uncertain waters."

"I'm just saying, Shelby—he's a Mercer. His family is philanthropic and all that but they're also ruthless when it comes to business."

Shelby's stomach twisted. "Babies are hardly business."

"To Mercers?" her mother said. "Maybe they are."

Shelby frowned and was afraid she was going to burst into tears so she gripped the door handle.

"Honey, I'm not trying to scare you. I'm just trying to tell you to keep your guard up. Okay?"

Shelby hugged her mother, the tears pricking, anyway. "Oh, trust me. My guard couldn't be up higher."

Suddenly, three Ingallses were hugging her and then Shelby picked up Shane's carrier and left, her heart so heavy she had to stop three times to catch her breath on the ten-minute walk to her apartment.

Chapter Five

As Liam pulled up into a spot in front of Treasures, he glanced up at the two-story brick building, lights glowing from behind curtains in the apartment windows above the shop. He had no idea how he was going to live in this tiny apartment with a woman who stole the air around him because she was so vital to him and with two babies who each made his heart stop for very different reasons.

He'd make it work. To have Alexander and Shane both living with him, anything would be worth it.

He made five trips from the car to the side doorway that led directly up to the apartment, then rang the bell.

When Shelby opened the door, he was again struck by how moved he was. Not just because she was so pretty, her face scrubbed clean, her blond hair pulled back into a ponytail, jeans and a yellow hoodie on her tall, lean form. When he looked at Shelby Ingalls, even when he just thought about her, he felt rooted in the world, which was nuts. He'd just met the woman.

But their lives, the most important thing in their worlds, were now so entwined that he wanted to be connected to Shelby at all times. Must be why he was okay with moving into this little, strange place above a dusty shop full of old things. He could have insisted on them all moving to his ranch house, which had even too much room for four people, especially when two of them were itty-bitty. But this was Shelby's domain and he wanted to be in it.

She was Shane's mother. The mother of his biological son. And she was the biological mother of Alexander. His life.

"I'm not sure my apartment is big enough for all that," Shelby said with a smile as she looked down.

"Well, I had to take Alexander's rocking bassinet— he sleeps it in like a champ. And his favorite bouncer seat. And his tummy time mat. And the lullaby player. A few packs of diapers, wipes, his clothes, pj's, favorite blankets, stuffed animals and chew toys, and I'm a walking baby store."

Shelby laughed. "I'll help lug it. First, let me take this little guy up." She smiled at Alexander. "You're going to like the apartment," she whispered to the sleeping baby as she took his carrier. "Your buddy is up there and you're going to share his nursery. I painted the stars on the ceiling myself."

Liam loved how sweet she was to Alexander, how she talked to him, the catch in her voice. He wanted to take the carrier out of her hands and just hold her for a few minutes right here in the illumination of the overhead light, tell her this new beginning was going to work out fine. But instead, he grabbed the bulky exersaucer and followed her through a side door that led directly up a flight of stairs to the second floor and bypassed the need to go through the shop. *Focus on why you're here—the babies*, he told himself. *And stop focusing on Shelby herself.* "I told him all about the nursery on the way over."

She glanced behind her, that smile lighting up the dimly lit stairwell. "Did he say anything back?"

"He said he can't wait to be Shane's roomie."

Shelby laughed and went into the nursery, where she left Alexander in his carrier for the meantime, and Liam put the exersaucer in the living room. They raced back downstairs. She grabbed the two garment bags, which held his suits for work, and Liam took the bassinet and two duffels. Three trips later, everything was inside.

"Well, Alexander is fast asleep in his bassinet," Liam said as they stood in the nursery.

"Shane, too," she said, reaching into his crib to caress his little head.

They backed out of the room, leaving the door just slightly ajar. He followed Shelby into the living room and sat beside her on the big overstuffed red couch. He liked the apartment more than he'd expected. It was both soothing and colorful, cozy and practical, particularly with a baby living here—correction, two babies—and just plain inviting. He was used to his ranch with its brown leather couches and more stark furnishings, but he liked it here.

"I told my family what's going on," she said when

she came from the kitchen with a tray holding two mugs of coffee.

Liam added cream and sugar and took a sip of the needed hot brew. "Did they react like mine?"

She smiled. "Not quite, but they did warn me to be careful."

"Careful?"

"The Mercer name carries a lot of weight, Liam. You know that."

He put down his mug and took both her hands in his. "I'm going to say this again, Shelby. As many times as I need to. I will not do anything to hurt you. I will not attempt to take Shane away from you. I can't say it any more black-and-white than that. And I hope you won't attempt to take Alexander from me."

The relief that came over her must have been very strong because she flung her arms around him, and he held her tightly, resting his cheek against the top of her head. "We're in this together, Shelby."

She nodded, then pulled away. "I feel better." She tucked her legs underneath her and picked up her mug of coffee. "You weren't married to Alexander's mother?"

Liza's face floated into his mind and he tried to push it out. He couldn't think about Liza without feeling a hard punch of guilt.

He shook his head. "We only dated for a few weeks. My cousin Clara wanted to adopt a dog, so we went to the animal shelter to check them out. Liza worked there. That's how we met."

She smiled. "Did your cousin adopt a dog?"

"Sure did. She went in wanting a dog that didn't shed, bark and was completely trained in every regard. She left with a German shepherd mutt she fell in love with at first sight. He sheds, barks and is only a quarter trained. Meaning he'll do anything you say for a rawhide bone. His name is Bixby and now she has about a hundred lint rollers."

"I've always wanted a dog, but I inherited Luna from my grandmother five years ago and I don't think she'd appreciate a dog in the place."

"Ah, so that's what that black-and-white fuzzy thing I almost tripped over was—your cat."

Anything to delay talking about Liza. And how he'd let her down.

She smiled. "So you met Liza at the shelter…" Shelby prompted.

So much for changing the subject. "We were as different as night and day, but I liked her a lot. She was a real free spirit, into hiking and nature. She couldn't believe she fell for a corporate stooge."

Shelby smiled. "I totally get it."

"Well, somehow, we connected. We spent a lot of time together. She liked being out at my ranch, despite the lack of animals. Just to breathe in all that country Wyoming air. But then honesty came between us."

"Honesty?" she asked, wrapping her hands around her mug.

"We were talking about what we wanted from life, and I told her I had no intention of ever getting married or having children. That I was a lone wolf."

He paused, that hot poke of guilt stabbing at his gut.

He felt Shelby staring at him but didn't want to give her time or room to ask questions, so he rushed on. "I mean, I liked Liza. A lot. But I also liked things as they were. No commitment. Just two people enjoying each other's company. No rules, no musts. Because she was a free spirit, I thought she'd understand."

"But she didn't?"

He frowned, remembering the look on Liza's face. Disappointment. Hurt. "She told me that just because she was a free spirit didn't mean she didn't believe in love or forever, that in fact, love was everything to her. She said she wanted five kids. She asked me again if I was absolutely sure, if I could say with conviction that I never wanted to get married or have children. I said yes. I was sure. So she ended things."

He put his mug down and turned away a bit, resting his elbows on his knees, his head bowed. He hated this part of the story.

"The night she gave birth was the first time I'd heard from her in about seven, eight months. She called me on her way to the clinic and told me she was nine months pregnant with my baby, in labor, and she was sorry she hadn't told me. She said if anything happened to her, she left me a letter."

He stood up and walked to the windows, staring through the filmy embroidered curtains at Main Street in the dark, the familiar landmarks somehow comforting. There was the general store with its weather vane and silver cowboy hat atop it. The small library his mother had funded. He could just make out the Pie Diner at the tail end of the street, Pie Diner flanked by two painted wood pies, a cowboy lassoing one. He closed his eyes and kept hearing Liza's voice.

I'm nine months pregnant with your child.

And the words in her letter.

I'd never want my child to have a father who's not interested in him or her, a father who doesn't want the responsibility. That's why I didn't tell you. If anything happens to me, Liam, you'll be the baby's only parent, his or her only family. I have no one else, as you know. We only knew each other a few weeks, but I know you're a good person and caring and will step up if need be. Since need be is all I'll have, I'll take it. This is your child. That's all you need to know to love him. But I guess you'll have to find that out for yourself.

"If I'd known she was pregnant, I would have been there for her, making sure she had what she needed. Instead, she went through her pregnancy alone and she had no family. She was all alone, Shelby."

There it was. People let each other down. People could not be trusted, period. Even if you thought you meant well, you ended up breaking someone's heart, ruining a year or two of their life, scarring them. He'd been hurt. He'd done the hurting. It never ended. He'd vowed not to hurt Shelby because he wasn't romantically involved with her, never would be, despite how badly he wanted to kiss her, and could keep a solid emotional distance. As long as he kept her at arm's length, everything would be fine. So he would.

She got up and walked over to him, touching the back of his shoulder. "She wasn't alone, Liam. Not really. She had her baby. When I was pregnant and here by myself, I'd just touch my belly and I'd feel better. I'll bet Liza felt that way, too."

He appreciated that. He relaxed a bit, the knots in his shoulders—particularly the spot where she'd touched him—loosening. He let his mind wander to how Shelby would feel in his arms. He wanted her in his arms.

Arm's length, he reminded himself. That meant no touching her. No holding her.

"You planned to *never* marry or have kids?" she asked, heading back to the couch.

He turned around and sat down next to her, picking up his mug of coffee, and took a sip, wrapping his hands around the warmth of the cup. "I used to feel differently, years ago when I was young and naive. But no—I'm done with the idea of love and marriage. The kid situation took care of itself."

"So you adapted to parenthood, Liam. Maybe you could adapt to marriage. How could you be so sure you couldn't?"

"Because love doesn't last."

"My parents were married for twenty-two years until my father died. They were deeply in love until my father's last breath."

He glanced at her. "I'm sorry about your father."

"Love does last," she said. "It *does*. Or it can. Even if it hasn't for me."

"Or for me, Shelby. Twice I got my heart handed back to me in shards. I learned to not get emotionally invested. It's better that way." *And given the way I ended up failing Liza when she needed me?* Yes, he was done.

Shelby tilted her head at him, those green eyes regarding him. "I've never seen anyone more emotionally invested in another person than you with Alexander."

"He's my son. Not my girlfriend. And I don't have girlfriends anymore. Just dates here and there, three-week-long relationships where everything is clear and ends with no one disillusioned."

She picked up a cookie from the plate on the coffee table and took a bite. "You're a hard one. Are your parents happily married?"

He shrugged. "Honestly, it's hard to tell. Their marriage was all but arranged by my late grandmother, Alexandra. Alexander was named for her. She was something else. A brilliant businesswoman. My grandfather was smart and made her president of the company when the company started failing under his watch. She turned it around. She ran Mercer Industries and the family. My father really respected her. So when she pushed him to marry my mother, he complied. I guess they're happy enough. But their marriage certainly didn't make me think love is real or lasting or a reason to marry."

"A reason to marry?" Shelby repeated. "Love is the only reason!"

"There's also practicality."

"Well, I'm all for being practical and smart about how I live my life, but love and emotion can't be bullet-pointed in a memo about how to live."

He laughed. "Sure it can. I make bullet-pointed to-do lists every day. Today's got blown to bits, of course."

"See? Life works that way."

"Don't I know it, Shelby."

She glanced at him, then sipped her coffee, her gaze landing on the brown bag his mother had given her at dinner. She jumped up and brought it back to the sofa. "It was nice of your mom to give it to me for Treasures."

"It was thoughtful. Larrisa Mercer can be very kind and loving. She can also be very, very practical."

Shelby reached in and lifted out a medium-size something wrapped in newspaper. She unwrapped it, stuffing the paper back in the bag on the floor. She gasped as she examined it. "Wow, it's absolutely beautiful! I can't believe your mother didn't want this." She turned it around in her hands, the ornately jeweled tin box sparkling when it caught the light from the floor lamp. She reached underneath and twisted the metal prong, Mozart playing softly. "Lovely. Honestly, I want it for myself."

He smiled. "Keep it, then."

"I love mysteries, don't you? Don't you wonder who dropped it off on your parents' porch and why?" She leaned down and scooped up the bag, looking at his father's name scrawled across it, then put it back down. "As your mother said, maybe your father once did the person a favor and this is a thanks."

"My father doesn't do favors unless there's one coming back."

She frowned at him and opened the lid. The box was about six by eight and lined in an unexpected pink velvet. Shelby smiled. "This is definitely not for sale. I'm going to keep it as a memento of the first time I met your family. The day I met you."

"It's been one hell of a Friday."

She laughed. "Sure has."

"Let's add Saturday to the mix, too, then," he said. "Let's go talk to the nurse who switched our babies."

Shelby turned to him, putting the jewelry box back in the bag. "Should we wait until we have the DNA results?"

"I feel like I'll go out of my mind if I don't have information, something, to help explain where we are now. Shane can't be your biological child. Something has to account for that. And it has to be the nurse."

Shelby nodded slowly, her expression so pained that he regretted his words, that Shane couldn't be her child. He was.

He reached for her hand. "I'm sorry this happened, Shelby."

"Me, too. Except—and this is going to sound crazy—if it hadn't happened I wouldn't have Shane. I wouldn't have loved this little boy for the past six months. Granted, I wouldn't have known otherwise. But how can I regret having loved Shane all this time?"

He wanted to pull her to him and tell her he knew exactly what she meant. But he held back.

"Let's go talk to the nurse in the morning," she said. "I want to hear what happened but I'm scared, too. That she'll take any last, lingering bit of hope away. That somehow, this is all a mistake and Shane is mine and Alexander is yours."

"I know," he said. "I know."

In the middle of the night, Shelby woke up to the sound of a baby crying, and the different strain to the cries made her rush into the nursery. But it wasn't Shane crying. It was Alexander. And Liam was already there, soothing him on the rocker.

Half-naked.

Shelby was suddenly aware that she was wearing a tank top and yoga pants and showing more than she'd planned to her new housemate. *Note to self: from now on, grab bathrobe.*

"He's settling down," Liam said. "Maybe cutting his first tooth. I think I saw a little white nub on his gum."

"Shane cut his first just last week," she said, coming over and caressing Alexander's silky brown hair. His mouth quirked and his one hand shot up in a fist, then he scrunched his mouth around until he finally settled down, fast asleep. She smiled.

"Sorry we woke you," he said.

She was staring at his chest, she realized. His very muscular chest, dark hair whirling in the center. He wore sweats and was barefoot and he was so damned sexy that she had to look away.

"I'm used to it," she whispered, barely able to find her voice.

What she wasn't used to was a man in her apartment, taking care of business, taking care of a child. In the hours between her discovering she was pregnant and telling Shane's father the news, she'd had all these wonderful fantasies—fantasies that she thought would become reality. A scenario like this one, for example. Waking up to her baby's cries and rushing into the nursery only to find his father there first, holding their child, soothing him, rocking him back to sleep. And then the two grown-ups going back to their own room and making love, falling asleep spooned together, his arms around her. Shelby protected and safe in his love. She'd had those fantasies for just four hours before they were blown to bits.

Liam stood, and Shelby shook those thoughts away. She watched as he put Alexander in his crib and pressed a finger to his lips and then his son's cheek. "Sweet dreams," he whispered, and then they both quietly exited the room.

He stared at her for a good long moment, and she wondered what he was thinking.

God, I want to kiss him. That was her sudden thought.

Was he thinking the same about her?

Adrenaline and panic were at play, that was all. She had to keep her lips and hands to herself. This situation was hard enough without falling for a man who wasn't interested in marriage or family life, despite being a great dad.

"Well, good night," she said. "Next cry is mine."

He smiled and headed back to his room and the moment he disappeared from her sight she missed him.

Chapter Six

In the morning Liam sat on the bed in the guest room at Shelby's, distracted by the sounds of two babies gurgling and Shelby's melodic voice asking who wanted apricot baby food and who wanted peaches. Then he heard her saying they could both have a handful of their favorite cereal, Toasty Os. He heard Alexander babbling happily and Shelby moving about the kitchen, the cabinet doors closing, a chair scooting in.

He liked the gentle noise. He was used to living alone—well, with a baby, who said a couple of words that sounded like da and ba but otherwise babbled or cried or let out various levels of shrieks, happy or otherwise. Now, someone else—a woman—was taking care of Alexander this morning. It felt funny. And nice.

He'd gotten up the moment he heard a baby stir and

fuss—turned out to be Shane, and Shelby had beaten him into the nursery.

"I've got this," she'd said, a baby in each arm. "Relax, take a shower, have some coffee."

Relax? He couldn't even imagine. Not for a long time. He'd thanked her, taken his coffee to his bedroom and had gotten busy on the telephone. He'd started with Anne Parcells.

The Wedlock Creek Clinic's administrator hadn't been comfortable giving out the nurse's contact information, citing a pending internal investigation, so Liam did some investigating of his own and easily found her name and then her address. Kate Atwood on Cumberland Road.

Liam had then called Mrs. Atwood, explained who he was and why he wanted to talk to her, and she was reluctant and nervous. He'd explained that both he and Shelby felt a bit lost and thought hearing what happened, what may have happened, from the night nurse who'd been there would be a comfort or provide a sense of grounding. She'd finally agreed to have them over this morning at nine o'clock.

Liam headed back into the kitchen. Shelby was scooping scrambled eggs onto plates just as toast popped up in the red toaster on the counter. "I was just about to call you for breakfast. I have no idea how you like your eggs. If you like eggs."

"I love scrambled eggs. And toast. And thank you," he said.

"Bwa!" Shane babbled. Alexander eyed him and said, "Tawaba!"

Liam smiled. "From lonely onlys to brothers."

Shelby's entire face lit up. "I hadn't really thought

of that. But you're right." Her gaze on the boys was so tender, so reverent, so…happy that he almost slid an arm around her and held her close so they could both just stare at these magnificent tiny creatures they'd created. Everything Shelby was going through, he was going through. He'd never experienced anything like it before. Liam wasn't entirely sure, but he thought what was going on was called *intimacy*. Real, true intimacy. They understood each other on a level that was surprisingly comforting—and made him uneasy.

Which was why he changed the subject. He explained about the calls and their appointment with Kate Atwood. The beautiful moment they'd shared—gone. And he instantly felt less tense.

"I think we should go without the boys, though," Shelby said as she put a few more Toasty Os cereal on each baby's high chair. "I think that might be too much for the woman."

Liam topped off his coffee, which had to be his tenth in the past twenty-four hours. "You're right. She may feel more comfortable talking to us if we're not holding the babies she switched."

"I'm sure my mom and aunt would love to watch both boys," she said. "They'll be at the diner but can take turns keeping an eye."

"People eat pie for breakfast?" he asked. "I never thought of that."

"No one needs a reason or a time to eat pie. Our fruit pies are popular for breakfast, but my aunt Cheyenne makes five kinds of quiches for the breakfast crowd. Egg pie—with the most heavenly additions you can imagine. For dinner there are chicken pot pies, meat pies. Pie isn't just apple pie."

"I'll never think of pie the same way again."

She smiled. "They'll make you take a few boxes for the road. It's just how they are."

"Good. I don't turn down pie."

He could talk about pie for hours. Anything but switched babies and retired nurses and clinic blackouts.

"I'll call my mom," she said, reaching for her phone.

While she was on the phone, Liam entertained the babies with a little peekaboo. Shane didn't like when his face was hidden. But he got a big smile when he opened his hands from in front of his face and exclaimed, "Peekaboo! I see you!"

Shelby put her phone back on the counter. "We're all set. My mom said she can't wait to meet Alexander. Cheyenne and Norah, too."

"Why do I doubt that your mom will react like my father? I don't even know your mother but if she's anything like you, I can't imagine her referring to Alexander as her *real* grandson."

"Shane will always be her grandson. Alexander will feel like a bonus for a bit and then within a couple of weeks she'll forget that she didn't know he existed for the first six months of his life. Maybe that's how it'll be for your dad."

"We'll see. But I won't hold my breath."

They packed up the babies and drove over to the Pie Diner, just a quarter mile down Main Street and well situated next door to the library. The diner had been in business since Liam was a little kid, and his grandmother used to take him there all the time. Alexandra Mercer was no baker, but she loved pie. He'd never paid much attention to the menu and always ordered his favorite: Key Lime.

"I love how the place has changed over the decades but still has the same feel it always had," he said as they pulled into the gravel parking lot. He'd always liked the painted cowboy on a horse lassoing five painted wood 3D pies on the other side of the sign.

They barely got out of the car with the babies in their carriers when the door burst open and three women emerged, all various shades of blond with Pie Diner aprons on.

"I just saw you last night but I can't get enough of you," said the one Liam assumed was Shelby's mother. She was tall and slender like Shelby with chin-length blond hair and Shelby's green eyes. She took the carrier from Shelby and kissed Shane on his forehead. "Don't tell your mom but I'm gonna give you a little taste of apple filling this morning. Just wait till you get a real tooth and get through my amazing pie crust."

Liam smiled and extended his hand. "Liam Mercer. And this little guy is Alexander."

"Arlena Ingalls," she said, shaking his hand. "I'd pull you into a hug but we're both short a hand." She turned to Alexander in Liam's arms. "Hello, Alexander. You are absolutely adorable."

Shelby smiled. "And this is my aunt Cheyenne and my sister, Norah."

"Nice to meet you all," Liam said.

Cheyenne's long, curly hair blew forward in the breeze but she didn't brush it back from her face. She was staring from Shane to Liam, from Liam to Shane. "My God, Shane is the spitting image of you," she said to Liam, her hand covering her mouth.

"He is," Shelby's mother said with a nod.

Norah was looking from Alexander to Shane, then to Liam and Shelby. "And Alexander looks a lot like Shelby if you can ignore all that blond hair she has. It's in the eyes and the expression. And—he has the little Ingalls birthmark. Shelby has it. And so did our father."

Shelby nodded. "It all adds up to the babies being switched. That's why we have no doubt what the DNA tests will reveal. It may seem early to go talk to the nurse, but we just want to, need to."

"I can understand that," Norah said. "Was she nervous about the idea of meeting with you?"

Liam nodded. "I assured her we just need to talk to her off the record, nothing official, that this isn't about pointing fingers or looking to blame. It's just to understand, feel more connected to what happened."

"Well, you two take all the time you need," Shelby's mom said. "We're thrilled to watch both babies."

"Appreciate it," Liam said.

A few minutes later they were in Liam's SUV—alone. He looked in the back seat, sure he'd find Alexander and Shane back there, as usual, rear-facing in their seats. But just the bases were there. It was a funny feeling.

"Do you feel like we're missing something?" he asked.

She nodded. "I'm so used to having Shane with me at the shop that anytime he's not with me I feel like I lost something."

"You have a nice family. They seem like a very loving bunch."

She smiled. "They're in the pie business. It's a happy, loving thing."

"Happier and more loving than mergers and acquisitions and management, that's for sure."

"But you love your work?" she asked.

"I like it. I wouldn't say I love it. But I do love the family history, the tradition, to working on something started by my great-grandfather. I'm glad it's Saturday, though, so I don't have to have Mercer Industries on my mind. I put in a few hours on the weekends, but I try very hard to devote off time to Alexander."

She smiled. "You're a great dad."

He felt her compliment inside him. "Means a lot coming from a great mom."

That beautiful smile lit up the car again, and when a swath of her blond hair fell forward he was tempted to tuck it back away from her pretty face. He'd been so aware of her last night in the room right next door. He'd been tempted to get out of bed and pretend he heard Alexander fussing just so he could see her again, look at her, be with her. He wasn't sure how he'd feel about living in a small apartment above a shop, but the moment he'd arrived last night with his bags and Alexander's things, he'd felt at home because Shelby and Shane were there.

But he still didn't feel a connection to Shane yet. Maybe he'd need the DNA test results to make it feel real and then his heart would catch up with his head. Or maybe it would just take time. Just because Alexander wasn't his biologically didn't mean the baby was any less Liam's son. Liam had a feeling the space he was putting—emotionally—between himself and Shane was because of Shelby. At this point he wouldn't want her throwing herself into the role of Alexander's mother, just as he was sure she wouldn't want him to suddenly become Shane's father. They both had to move slowly—and were.

After fifteen minutes down a rural service road, Liam turned onto Berrymill Road and slowed down as he approached the yellow Cape Kate had told him to look out for. "Looks like we're here."

A woman stepped onto the porch. She was petite and looked haggard and tired, as though she hadn't slept in days. Or since yesterday.

"Ready?" Liam asked Shelby.

She nodded and they both got out of the car. Liam held up a hand to the woman, and they headed up the porch steps. Up close, Kate Atwood definitely showed even more signs of not sleeping. There were dark circles under her eyes, and she looked as if she might break down in tears at any minute. Liam's research had revealed she was sixty-six years old and she looked quite a bit older. She was petite and thin with short, light brown hair shot through with gray, and brown eyes behind glasses.

"Come on in," she said. "I've made iced tea and have homemade oatmeal cookies, if you like."

Shelby offered a gentle smile. "I never pass up a cookie. I come from a long line of bakers. Pie bakers, but I do love cookies."

Shelby's warmth clearly set the woman at ease. Liam watched Kate's shoulders relax and her entire countenance changed. She still looked like she might cry, but the fear that had been in her expression, as though they might turn their anger on her, lightened up some.

They followed her into a cozy living room. Liam and Shelby sat on the love seat across from the recliner that Kate took. She gestured at the cookies, the pitcher of iced tea and glasses. "Please help yourself."

They did, more to ease in to what was to come than thirst or hunger.

Shelby took a sip of tea, then put her glass down and clasped her hands. "Mrs. Atwood, we understand that you were the nurse on duty in the maternity area of the clinic the night our babies were born. As you know, the clinic administrator has informed me that my son Shane can't be the baby I gave birth to. We're awaiting DNA testing but all signs do point to the two male babies being accidentally switched. Can you tell us what happened? What you remember?"

Kate looked at each of them and took a deep breath. "First, I am so sorry." Tears glistened in her eyes. "When Anne called me and had me come in to discuss that night, I had no inkling that I might have switched two babies. But when she said that one baby couldn't be the biological child of one of the mothers, I immediately knew that I must have switched the two male newborns."

"Can you tell us what was happening at that time?" Liam asked.

Kate folded and unfolded her hands in her lap. "It was terrible. The wind was howling so badly and we were all so afraid the power could go out and it did. The generator came on but then it failed, too. I'd just brought the Ingalls baby to the nursery to weigh and measure him and the lights came back on so I put him in the bassinet and ran to Ms. Harwood's labor and delivery room for her infant to bring him to the nursery.

The lights went out again just as I approached. All of a sudden, a tree fell on the east wing and people were screaming in fear. I put the Harwood baby down in a bassinet for safety and wheeled both over away from the windows. I was sure the Ingalls baby was on the left and the Harwood baby was on my right. But in the chaos, I must have mixed them up. I must have put the bracelets on the wrong babies."

"You said you had no inkling you might have switched the babies," Liam said gently. "As you were braceleting them, you didn't think for a second that you could have switched them?"

She shook her head. "I was so sure. Ingalls left, Harwood right. And I remembered thinking, the Harwood baby had that tiny birthmark on his right ear."

"Like this," Shelby said numbly, pointing at her own ear.

"If only the lights hadn't gone out the moment Shane was born," Liam said. "Shelby would have noticed the birthmark—and noticed that it was gone when she next held her baby. Because she was holding the wrong infant."

"I'd mixed them up in my mind even before I put on their bracelets," Kate said. "How could I have done such a thing? I'd been a nurse for over thirty years. I am so, so sorry for what I did. I take full responsibility."

Liam looked at Shelby. He watched her get up and go sit down next to the retired nurse and put her arms around her. The woman looked so surprised that she burst into tears and held tightly on to Shelby.

"It was an honest mistake in the chaos of a terrible snowstorm," Liam said. "It happened and that's that.

Nothing's going to undo it so we just all have to accept it and move on."

Kate wiped under her eyes with a tissue. "You sure are being kind about this. My daughter said we should expect to be sued."

"No one is suing anyone, Kate," Liam said. "I want you to put that worry out of your head."

The woman burst into tears again, covering her face with her hands.

"Kate?" someone called from upstairs. "Is it time for my soup? Where is my soup?"

Kate took a breath. "That's my mother. She's elderly and not very well."

"We won't take any more of your time," Liam said. "Thanks for meeting with us."

"Yes, thank you," Shelby said. "It was helpful to hear what happened. How it happened."

Kate walked them to the door, her mother calling about her soup again. "Are you going to switch the babies back?"

Shelby froze.

Liam felt momentarily sick.

It was the first time anyone had actually asked that question.

"No, ma'am," Liam said. "I have a better idea."

Shelby glanced at him, questions in her eyes.

"Where is my soup!" Kate's mother called again.

"You go ahead, Kate," Shelby said, stepping out onto the porch. "Thanks for talking to us."

Kate nodded and shut the door behind them.

Liam leaned his head back and he headed down the porch steps. "I need about ten cups of coffee or a bottle of scotch."

"I thought I might fall over when she asked about switching the babies back," Shelby said, her face pale, her green eyes troubled. She stared at him. "You said you had a better idea. What is it? I sure need to hear it. Because switching the babies is not an option. Right?"

"Damned straight it's not. Never will be. Shane is your son. Alexander is my son. No matter what. Alexander will also become your son and Shane will also become my son as the days pass and all this sinks in."

"I think so, too," she said. "Right now it's like we can't even process that babies we didn't know until Friday are ours biologically. But as we begin to accept it, I'll start to feel a connection to Alexander. Same with you and Shane."

He nodded. "Exactly. Which is why on the way here, I started thinking about a way to ease us into that, to give us both what we need and want."

She tilted her head, waiting.

He thought he had the perfect solution. The only solution.

"I called the lab running the DNA tests and threw a bucket of money at them to expedite the results. On Monday," he continued, "we will officially know for absolute certain that our babies were switched. Of course we're not going to switch them back. I'd sooner cut off my arm."

"Me, too," Shelby said, staring at him. "So what's your plan?"

"The plan is for us to get married."

Shelby's mouth dropped open. "What? We've been living together for a day. Now we're getting married. Legally wed? Till death do us part?"

Liam opened Shelby's car door, and she got in, her entire body feeling like rubber. He shut the door and came round and got in. "Let's get out of here and talk. We'll go to my ranch. Then we'll pick up the boys."

She nodded, all she could manage. Married? What?

"On Monday we'll know with certainty, Shelby. You have my child and I have yours. You've been raising my son and I've been raising yours. You love Shane and I love Alexander. If we marry, if we join together as a family unit, we each have the boys we've been raising and the baby we didn't know was ours."

"Join together as a family unit," she repeated. "So… we're getting married to become a family. For the boys' sake and ours."

"Yes. Precisely."

Her baby's father floated into her mind. *One day we'll get married and it'll be us against the world. We'll have a big old house in the country, a chicken coop, maybe even horses. We'll watch reality TV and go to the rodeo and die old, fat and happy.*

They'd gotten married at the famed Wedlock Creek Chapel. Legend said that those who married at the chapel would have multiples in some way, shape or form: twins, triplets, quadruplets, even quintuplets, whether through nature, science, marriage, or adoption. The town and county was full of big families with identical twins and fraternal triplets. Morgan Crawford had said he'd hoped they'd have quintuplets. Except by the time she did discover she was pregnant, Morgan had two other girlfriends. One of whom was the supposed real love of his life. When Shelby, who had no clue her new husband was cheating on her, told him she was pregnant, he said he was sorry but he was filing for divorce and that, "I'm sorry, Shel, but happiness has to come first."

She was around six months along when she'd heard he'd died in a car wreck. Shelby had been very sad about the whole sorry story for so long that her sister had moved in with her for two weeks and made her scrambled eggs and toast every morning and minded the shop, letting her just lie on her sofa, her hands on her growing belly, unsure what anything meant anymore. If you couldn't trust the word of the man you loved, the man you thought loved you, the man you'd *married*, what could you believe in?

Heck, she couldn't even believe in the legend of the Wedlock Creek Chapel. She was pregnant with *one* baby, which was more than fine with her. But maybe true love and legends only came true for others.

You believe in this, Norah had said, taking Shelby's hands and putting them on her stomach, where she'd felt a good, hard kick. That kick had made her burst into a smile, her first in weeks, and from that moment on, she'd been fine. She had her baby-to-be. She had her family. She had Treasures. Her trust had been breached, but who said she had to let another man into her life? She certainly didn't plan to. Not for a long while, anyway.

Now here was Liam Mercer proposing they marry for the most practical of reasons. Maybe she shouldn't pooh-pooh it, no matter how much she believed that love, deep, abiding, lasting love, was real and waiting for her. Right now her heart was guarded with barbed wire.

But marry a man without love as the main reason? Come on.

"Think about it," he said. "I think it's a good solution. The only solution, really."

"But what about the future? What about love, Liam?"

He snorted. "Love? That's for fairy-tale endings. No—I take it back. I do love Alexander. And I'm going to love Shane the moment I let myself go and trust me, I've been fighting it."

She felt herself go limp. "I know. Me, too."

"Monday, the results will say that Shane is my flesh and blood. And the floodgates are going to open, Shelby. I think the same will happen to you."

"I know it will."

He pulled over and put the SUV in Park and turned to face her, reaching for her hand. "So, let's have our children. Both children. Together. A family unit."

She noticed he kept saying a family unit instead of a family. Because family implied something else, whereas a family unit sounded more like a business term. Because this would be a businesslike marriage. A merger, a spousal acquisition for the benefit of both parties. And both minor parties.

"I will think about it, Liam. But I won't give you an answer until I see the DNA results."

"Understood."

He put the car in Drive and continued on, signaling for the service road that would lead back into town.

Marriage. To Liam Mercer.

Chapter Seven

Shelby had needed a break from their conversation, so instead of going back to Liam's ranch to talk, they picked up the babies and each went their separate ways with the plan to meet up for dinner at home—home being Shelby's apartment. When Liam had dropped her and Shane off, he hadn't mentioned the proposal, and she'd gotten out of the car so fast it was a wonder she hadn't dropped Shane on his head. Maybe getting married was a ridiculous idea. But it seemed the only good one. The only solution to one hell of a situation.

"How about we go see the goats at Grandma and Grandpa's?" Liam said to Alexander as they pulled onto Main Street.

Of course from his rearview mirror he only had a view of the back of the baby's rear-facing car seat, but he still imagined Alexander smiling and clapping his hands about going to see the goats. As for Liam, he needed the open air and the hundreds of acres of wild Wyoming land. His own property had almost a hundred acres but was closer to town and more developed than his parents' place twenty miles out. Besides, he needed a sense of familiarity, of grounding about who he was.

He also wanted his father to show him that Harrington Mercer was back to being the loving, doting grandfather he'd always been. He didn't like being on the outs with his dad; they'd always gotten along, and Liam had always prided himself on understanding his father when his brother wouldn't even try. He'd stuck up for Harrington Mercer in arguments with Drake so many times over the years. But the way his father had thrown around words like *real grandson* had sent shock waves through his gut. He didn't like it and he needed that nonsense over and done with. He was sure his father would be back to his old self today now that he'd had some time.

As he pulled up in the circular drive, Harrington Mercer was just coming back from the stable, his usually perfectly coiffed salt-and-pepper thick hair a bit mussed, which meant he'd been out riding.

"Thought I'd show your grandson the goats," Liam said as he got out of the car and took out Alexander. He turned toward the penned pasture where around ten goats of all colors were grazing.

"Sure," Harrington said, his voice strained. Liam noticed he didn't reach for Alexander. Or say one word to him, as a matter of fact. "Your mother and I have a fund-raising dinner, so just see yourself out when you're done here."

Alexander reached out his hands for his grandfather, whom he adored. "Ga," he said, one of his only words.

Harrington glanced at the baby. "I'd better hit the showers." With that he turned and walked away.

"Stop right now," Liam said, his voice so cold it surprised even him. "Your grandson is reaching for you."

"I just told you—"

"I know what you said, Dad. I want to hear what you're *not* saying."

"I'm preparing myself, okay?" Harrington said, a mix of anguish and resolve in his eyes. "You're expecting the DNA tests soon. They're going to say that Alexander isn't a Mercer. That he's not my grandson. I need to prepare for that, Liam. I need to take a step back."

Liam's legs actually buckled. He expelled a breath and tried to collect himself, to get over the sharp left hook his brain just took. "Not a Mercer? Not your grandson? Dad, he was your grandson two days ago. He's your grandson now. He'll be your grandson Monday, no matter what the hell the DNA tests say."

"The DNA results will say he's that Ingalls woman's child. He's her baby. He's her father's grandson."

Liam sucked in a breath. "And *that Ingalls woman's* child—Shane? On Monday is he suddenly going to become your grandson?"

"I suppose he is. I'll have to work that out in my own time, get to know him."

"Dad, Alexander is your grandson and will always be. Just as he'll always be my son."

"That's not how life works, Liam."

"It damn well is." He looked at Alexander for a long moment, then turned and walked away.

Red-hot anger was working its way up every nerve in Liam's body. He stomped back to his SUV, put Alexander back inside as gently as he could given his mood and peeled out of there. Ten minutes ago he'd needed this land, the place he'd grown up, to soothe him, to ground him. Now he never wanted to step foot here again.

Shelby wrapped the adorable elephant salt-and-pepper shakers in pink tissue paper, put them in a Treasures bag and handed it over to her smiling customer. The woman had actually left five minutes earlier with a pricey tea set that Shelby had found at an estate sale a few weeks ago, but she'd returned, unable to stop thinking about the shakers. Her customers often did that. And that was how the heart worked. You might pass something up, but if you couldn't stop thinking about it, especially a minute after leaving, you had to come back and make it your own.

This afternoon had been good for business. Her sister, Norah, had filled in for her this morning while she and Liam had been out to see Kate Atwood. Shelby usually told Norah everything, but she found herself holding back the bit about the marriage proposal. Shelby could barely wrap her mind around it.

And she was grateful that the shop had been busy all day. Between answering questions about the origin of pieces—she usually had no idea—and whether lightbulbs came with the lamps—no—and if she'd go down ten dollars on the price—usually, since she expected to be asked—she'd barely had time to think about Liam's proposal. Marriage.

Her gaze landed on the brown paper bag that Liam's mother had given her last night; she'd brought it down to examine it further during slow times, and there was finally a lull. She glanced at Shane, napping in his bouncer seat behind the gated register area, then excitedly reached in the bag and pulled out the wrapped box, quickly taking off the newspaper.

The music box was so beautiful. And so old. Shelby guessed it was at least a hundred years old and had been passed down from generation to generation. She ran her hand on the pretty pink velvet lining, worn with use, and she imagined what had been in this box over the decades—brooches and earrings and pearl necklaces, beloved treasures. As her fingertip brushed the far edge of the lining, she realized there was something underneath. She tugged at the side and it released easily. The lining had a smooth edge that would easily tuck back under.

Under the lining was a folded-up piece of paper!

A secret note? A love letter? Should she read it or tuck it back and leave the writer the privacy he or she had expected by hiding it under the lining?

But the music box had ended up in her possession. So maybe it was okay to read it. Just the first line or two, and if it belonged to someone she knew she'd stop reading immediately and return it.

The bell jangled, and Shelby looked up. Liam. Looking absolutely awful. Well, looking absolutely gorgeous but angry. He was pacing, Alexander in his baby carrier, fast asleep.

Secret note, you will have to wait until later. She

tucked it back under the lining and put the music box back in the bag and stowed it under her desk, lest anyone think the box was for sale.

"You okay?" she asked. He clearly wasn't.

Steam was practically coming out of his ears. "My father doesn't think of Alexander as his grandson anymore. He's not a Mercer anymore, apparently. He's an Ingalls."

Shelby froze, the idea of that innocent baby being rejected by his grandfather too much to take in. "What?"

As three women came in to browse, Shelby smiled tightly at them, then took Liam's hand and pulled him closer to the wall. "Not his grandson? What?"

She watched his face as he told her what happened at his parents' house. So many emotions flashed—fury, hurt, bewilderment.

"No one turns their back on my son. Especially not my father," he growled under his breath.

"Alexander is your son, no matter what," she said. "And as you told your father, he always will be, also no matter what. What you feel for him is in here—" she added, touching her heart. "That won't change because of DNA."

"Well, apparently my father is heartless. That's the only excuse I can think of."

Except from what Liam had told her of his father, Harrington Mercer wasn't heartless. Why would he shun the baby he loved so much? It made no sense.

She reached for Liam's hand. "I'm so sorry. He must be going through some major adjustment issues over this. I'm sure he'll come around."

"Adjustment issues? He doesn't get the right. The

situation is what it damned well is," he added on a harsh whisper. "Accept it and carry on. That's the only way to go."

"Maybe you're a lot stronger than he is, Liam. Maybe he just needs time."

"I don't care what he needs," he snapped. He stopped, leaned his head back and let out a breath, then looked at her. "Sorry. I don't mean to take this out on you. I need to go upstairs, put Alexander down for his nap and take a hot shower. I could use some time to myself so it's good that you need to work. See you at closing."

She nodded and gave him something of a commiserating smile and her heart went out to him as he trudged past her, hurt and anger so evident in his eyes.

Dammit.

An hour and forty minutes until closing. For a moment Shelby considered turning the open sign to closed and locking up for the day. Time alone or not, Liam needed her. But the Minnow sisters walked in just then.

"Missed you yesterday," Callie said, her emerald silky scarf lovely against her hazel eyes.

"We waited a half hour, but you never opened," Bea added. "We were so worried. I hope you're okay."

She smiled at the three kind elderly sisters. "I'm fine. I just had something unexpected to attend to and it went on a bit longer than I thought it would. Sorry about that. But come on in and look around. I did put some new things out. June," she said to the only redhead among the blonde sisters, "I found a wonderful framed old map of Wyoming from the turn of the last century. I know you love old maps."

The women excitedly began looking at the merchandise, June beelining for the art wall.

For the next fifteen minutes, she vaguely listened as the sisters talked about the history of Wedlock Creek, one eye on the cuckoo clock and the other at the door, which kept opening as post-rodeo Saturday shoppers came in.

In the next hour alone, Shelby made over four hundred dollars. Not bad at all. But nothing was worth thinking of Liam upstairs alone, stewing, hurt, angry. Finally, six o'clock chimed, and Shelby flipped the sign, grabbed Shane's carrier and headed upstairs. It wasn't until she'd unlocked the apartment door that she realized she'd left the music box downstairs behind the counter. Drat. She'd come back for it later. Now all she wanted was to talk to Liam.

She didn't hear a sound when she entered the apartment. She headed into the nursery and saw Alexander sleeping in his bassinet. She lowered Shane into his crib and kissed his forehead, then began tiptoeing out, her ears straining for any sign of Liam. The apartment was dead quiet.

It was only when she was about to walk through the nursery doorway when she spotted him, again deliciously half-naked in a pair of navy sweats on the glider chair in the corner, a book about a talking pear open on his lap. He was asleep, the dim lighting casting shadows on his handsome face.

She fought the urge to curl up on his lap and listen to his heartbeat, which was what she wanted to do. Their children were in this room. Liam was in this room.

Her heart was in this room.

She was falling in love with him.

The truth hit her upside the head to the point that she had to put her hand on the doorknob to steady her legs. *Yes, I'm falling in love with you*, she said to his beautiful, sleeping form. *You're caring and kind and a great dad and you've shown me so much consideration and tenderness. And God, look at you*, she thought, her gaze going from all that silky, thick, dark hair to his long eyelashes resting at the tops of his cheeks, the chiseled jawline with just a hint of five o'clock shadow, the strong neck and broad shoulders and that chest, muscular and practically hairless, the waistband of his sweats covering long legs. Even his bare feet were sexy.

She was going to marry this man? This man who didn't believe in love and had proposed a marriage for circumstances' sake? Try as she might not to consider his proposal, she'd thought about it constantly. It did seem like the only solution. They would be a family unit. No one would lose anything. The babies would have their parent and their biological parent, and Liam and Shelby would have their sanity.

But would she really? Or would she go absolutely bonkers? She was already feeling too much for Liam Mercer. What if she fell whole hog in love with him and he made it even more crystal clear that this wasn't a romantic union, that love had nothing to do with it?

This isn't about your love life, dope, she reminded herself. *It's about keeping Shane and raising Alexander. It's about the babies. It's about keeping your heart intact.*

Yes, she would remember that. The whole point of marrying Liam Mercer was so that she would have both babies and not have her heart shredded. If she kept that vital point at the forefront, she would remember that that was where her heart had to lie—with the boys. Not the man.

I will marry you, Liam Mercer. If I got through that meeting on Friday morning with the Wedlock Creek Clinic administrator, I can get through anything.

She'd let him know on Monday—when the results came in.

Liam woke up just about every hour on the hour Sunday night, the anticipation of tomorrow too much for his brain to handle. He already knew, intellectually, that Alexander wasn't his biological son and that the DNA test would reveal that Shane was. But he still couldn't wrap his mind around it, believe it on a gut level.

He cursed and threw the blanket off and got out of bed, trying to be as quiet as possible. He needed a shot of whiskey. Something to turn his brain off and get him back to sleep.

The kitchen light was on, and he slowly approached, not sure if Shelby would want company at 3:12 in the morning. For a moment he stood in the doorway and just watched her, sitting at the round table by the window, her hands wrapped around a blue cup, steam still emanating. She wasn't facing him, but he could see the tightness in her face, her jawline.

"You, too, huh?" he whispered.

She turned and nodded and then burst into tears.

"Shelby," he said, rushing over to her. He leaned down and put his arms around her, and she shot up and wrapped her arms around him, sobbing full force. "I know," he soothed. "I know exactly how you feel." He tightened his hold on her and let her cry, resting his head on top of hers. Her hair was silky and smelled like coconuts.

Talk about getting his mind off tomorrow. Who needed whiskey when there was beautiful, sweet Shelby smelling like the beach?

"It's going to be okay," he whispered. "We're going to make it okay. You and me. We're going to be a family, Shelby."

He felt her nodding her head against his chest, her sobs subsiding, her breathing ragged. She sucked in a breath and just stayed in his arms. He reached a hand to her hair and stroked the silky blond mass, then lifted her face to his.

"Everything is going to be okay," he repeated.

She looked up at him, and he could see she was trying to believe it, to make herself believe it. "Sometimes I'll believe anything you say, Liam."

"Now's the time. Because we're going to make it okay. We just have to remember that everything we do is to keep our children. To have the children we were denied. If we remember why we're here, why we're doing this, we'll keep what's important at the forefront."

"I want Shane and I want Alexander."

"I want Alexander and I want Shane," he said. "Getting married makes that happen. And it'll make it a lot easier if we need to formally adopt the babies we've been raising for six months and the ones we haven't been."

She nodded and wiped under her eyes, and he

pulled her close again. This time she just held on tightly, not saying anything.

The urge to kiss her was so overpowering that Liam loosened his hold on her. He wanted her so bad, to let his hands fall from around her shoulders down her back to her waist and up to her breasts.

Did he not just tell Shelby they had to focus on what was important: the children? Letting himself feel more for Shelby, giving in to his attraction for her, would make for a hot night, but would end up ruining everything down the line. Romance died. Love faded. People moved on. He and Shelby couldn't take the risk of a failed romance getting in the way of their family.

He pulled back and dropped his hold on her.

"Everything is going to be okay," she repeated, a wobbly smile on her face.

Now suddenly he wasn't so sure himself.

Chapter Eight

Monday was a rainy, chilly mess. Good, Liam thought, glancing out the window of the Wedlock Creek Clinic. The perfect kind of day for absolute proof that you walked out the clinic with someone else's baby. That someone else walked out with your baby.

He glanced at Shelby sitting next to him. She sat ramrod straight, staring ahead, the strain on her face unbearable to him. He reached a hand down to squeeze hers, and she glanced at him for a moment and squeezed back, then let go.

The moment of truth had arrived.

The administrator handed each of the attorneys, sitting on either side of them, a copy of the test results. She cleared her throat and from the way she closed and opened her eyes very quickly, he knew without a doubt what the results said.

"Ms. Ingalls, you are not the biological mother of Shane Ingalls," Anne Parcells said. "You are the biological mother of Alexander Mercer. Mr. Mercer, you are not the biological father of Alexander Mercer. You are the biological father of Shane Ingalls. Based on the findings and discussions with the nurse on duty the night of November 5, it is our understanding that the babies were, indeed, accidentally switched."

This time, Shelby gripped his hand and held on.

"I meant what I said," he whispered. "It's going to be okay. We have a plan. Let's both remember that and we'll get through this meeting."

She bit her lip and nodded, her hold tightening on his hand. He couldn't even say this was the worst moment, finding out with absolute certainty that Alexander was not his child. No, that honor went to the first meeting, in this office, when a part of his brain was trying to understand what the administrator was saying—that the two male babies born the night of November 5 had been switched. He'd never forget it, the way everything in him had seized up. There had been times in his life when the world, including his own personal one, didn't make sense. But nothing would ever come close to how he'd felt when Anne Parcells had implied the babies had been switched.

Liam's attorney whispered in his ear about whether or not he'd changed his mind about the lawsuit. He had not. Shelby's attorney, whom Liam had learned on the way over was actually her sister's new boyfriend, also whispered something in Shelby's ear. He watched her shake her head.

Liam stood. "I speak for both myself and Shelby Ingalls. There will be no lawsuit. There be no litigation of any kind against this clinic, which serves a vital purpose to our county, or against the nurse, Kate Atwood. A mistake was made during a raging snowstorm. It wasn't about negligence. It was about act-of-God chaos."

"I appreciate that, Mr. Mercer," Anne Parcells said, relief visible on her face.

"I suppose you two have some things to work out between you, then," David Dirk said, glancing from Shelby to Liam.

"Actually, we have worked things out privately," Shelby said.

Did that mean she would accept his marriage proposal? Liam sure hoped so.

"Very good," Dirk said. "Shelby, please know if you need my services, just call. I'm here for you."

Shelby nodded. "I appreciate that, David."

With that, he left. Liam's attorney clapped him on the back, tapped Alexander on the nose and left, too.

Liam and Shelby stood, said goodbye to the administrator and headed out, and it wasn't until his face met the air that he realized he'd been holding his breath. Shelby stood beside him, her blond hair whipping behind her in the breeze, her expression fierce and sad and resigned.

He put his arm around her. "My son, your son, our sons. Doesn't matter which one we're talking about."

He saw her eyes glisten before she nodded. "My son, your son, our sons."

He pressed a kiss to Alexander's forehead and held him close. Shelby was doing the same to Shane.

"I accept your proposal, Liam. The family unit marriage. I accept."

"Good," he said. "Good."

"I suppose we'll go to the town hall and have the mayor marry us? She can probably do it this week."

"Town hall or whatever you want. Shelby. If you want a church wedding or the Wedlock Creek Chapel or the backyard at your mom's or if you want to clear an aisle in Treasures, I'll marry you wherever and whenever will make you happy."

She stilled and stared at him. "Happy? That's not really part of this."

"This might not be the traditional kind of marriage, Shelby, but it's legal and binding and we're going to be saying vows. I want you to have the wedding you want. Not what feels appropriate for the situation— who even knows what kind of wedding that would be."

She tilted her head. Not the beautiful Wedlock Creek Chapel, that was for sure. Been there, done that. "A town hall wedding. But I'll think on it. And thank you. Once again, there you go showing me a very thoughtful, kind side of yourself."

"I know this isn't easy, Shelby. I know this can't be what you dreamed of when you dreamed about your wedding day. But let's make it as special as it deserves to be. We're each getting a new son, six months after the fact, who happens to be our flesh and blood. That damned well deserves a parade."

She hugged him with her free arm, and he was glad he made her feel better.

"What kind of wedding do *you* want?" she asked.

"As long as I'm marrying you, I don't much care otherwise."

She bit her lip and turned away. "Well, I'm going to see my family, to let them know the results. They're waiting on pins and needles."

She hurried away and he wanted her to come back. Her and Shane. "I'll see you at home in about an hour, okay? We'll plan it all out."

He nodded and he watched her as she settled Shane in her little silver car, then got in and drove off, taking two big pieces of himself with her.

"Wait," Norah said, forkful of Shelby's mocha chip pie in midair. "He said 'As long as I'm marrying you, I don't much care otherwise'?"

Shelby sat in the cushioned booth of her family's Pie Diner, Norah next to her, her mother and aunt Cheyenne across. The café was pretty busy but the moment the three women heard the words *I'm getting married* come out of Shelby's mouth, they rushed around to fill orders and coffee cups and slap down checks, then slid in, her sister stealing bites of her pie.

"But that sounds like he has feelings for you," Erin Ingalls said. "Are you sure he doesn't?"

"Very sure. He meant it as in, you're Alexander's biological mother and Shane's mother in all ways that matter. He didn't mean in the romantic sense. For a man who doesn't believe in love, I'm the only logical woman to marry based on the circumstances."

"Men who don't believe in love wouldn't marry at all," Aunt Cheyenne put in on a whisper, pointing to the two huge gossips who slid into the booth behind Shelby's.

"Well, the marriage won't be about love," Shelby reminded them. "Except the love of two six-month-old babies. We're joining as a family for our sakes and theirs."

"Don't tell me he's jetting you off to Vegas for a quick ceremony," Shelby's mom said. "This may be a marriage of circumstance but if my girl is getting married, I don't want to miss it."

Shelby smiled but it took some doing. "The whole thing is just so… I don't even know the right word. It's not a sham marriage. It's not a real marriage. It's just the only thing we can do. I don't know that a big celebration is in order."

"Well, it's certainly not temporary, either," Norah said. "Church wedding? Wedlock Creek Chapel? Reception in the backyard?"

Shelby did love her mother's backyard with its woods and trees and the pretty white lights hung across the deck railing. But a church wedding and a reception at home? No. That was just going too far. She thought again about the gorgeous Wedlock Creek Chapel where she'd married Morgan after their whirlwind courtship. She'd dreamed of marrying there and that dream had been spit on.

Huh. Maybe she could take back the dream. Get married at the chapel again. It wasn't as if she and Liam would be having sex, so the old legend about newlyweds being blessed with multiples wouldn't even have a chance to come true.

Her mind made up, Shelby finally dug into her pie. Mocha whip-chip pie—delicious. "I think the Wedlock Creek Chapel, and afterward we can take the boys to the park."

"I'm so glad you didn't choose the town hall," her mother said. "I know the marriage is just about paperwork and legalities. But it's still a ceremony. And there's no more beautiful place to marry than the chapel."

Shelby nodded. "Agreed. The marriage is definitely only about the legality. And then we'll start the paperwork to each adopt our biological baby. Liam is looking into whether we need to legally adopt the boys we took home, too."

Aunt Cheyenne shook her head. "What a thing." She rested her hand on Shelby's. "It may not be a love marriage, but Liam Mercer sounds like a good man, and you'll both have both boys."

Shelby nodded. "That's what's important. Not my love life. And we're both entering this marriage knowing what's what. So it's not like anyone can get hurt."

She caught her mother, aunt and sister glance at one another. Who was she kidding? Someone was going to get hurt and that someone was Shelby. Because she was falling in love with her fiancé. Getting married, living together as husband and wife, watching him be a father to their children, would only make her love him more.

You just have to put up a wall between you two, she told herself, sipping her coffee. But how?

"So, how's this going to work exactly?" Norah asked. She leaned forward and whispered, "I mean, once you're married, will you...?"

Shelby tilted her head. "What?" Three pairs of Ingalls green eyes stared at her with various glints of curiosity, amusement and wonder.

Ah.

They were talking about sex. About the bedroom.

"We haven't exactly talked about any of that stuff," Shelby said. "Guess we'd better."

"You two should square away on everything before the wedding," her mother said, getting up as a man could be heard muttering that the waitresses were sitting down on the job. "*Everything.* Make a list."

"What should be on it?" Shelby asked. "Besides the bedroom question."

"Well, that's number one," Norah said, sliding out of the booth and holding up a "gimme a minute" finger at a customer. "The rest you two need to come up with together."

As her family hugged her and got back to work, Shelby tried to think of what else they should get clear on, but everything was jumbled around in her head.

All she could really think about was that she was going to marry Liam Mercer. The handsome, kind man she'd been unable to stop thinking about last night as she lay in bed, her cat snuggled in a ball beside her. She knew what he slept in, just a pair of low-slung sweats, and it had been difficult to get his incredible body off her mind. And then she'd gotten out of bed to have some herbal tea and he'd come into the kitchen and she'd lost it.

She'd sobbed in his arms and he'd held her so close, making her believe what he was saying, that everything really would be okay. When they'd finally left the kitchen and gone back to their rooms, she'd wanted to slip inside his room with him, curl up beside him in bed, just to have his strong arms around her. But there would be no curling and cuddling in this union. Her dear cat would have to continue in that role.

A romance-free marriage, given the circumstances, was entirely appropriate. It was the way to go.

After what had happened with Shane's father, the way he'd become Dr. Jekyll and Mr. Hyde, Shelby hadn't been planning on falling for anyone for a good long time. Her plan had been to be a good mother, build her business and spend time with her family—people she knew she could trust no matter what.

Now here she was, about to marry a man she barely knew but had to trust and—God help her—did.

She just couldn't afford to love him. As if putting the brakes on love was possible. It might be for Liam Mercer, who seemed to have amazing powers of self-control. But a little part of her held out hope that even he wouldn't be able to stop love at full speed if what was blossoming between them grew into more.

Unless she was mistaking his kindness and concern for something else. She'd mistaken her ex's lying personality for sincerity. So maybe Shelby had better take a big step backward and focus on the family. The family *unit*, she amended.

Feeling stronger, more grounded and comfortable with moving forward, she took another bite of pie.

When Liam arrived back at Shelby's apartment from the Chinese restaurant with their take-out order, he froze and panicked with an *Oh, my God, I forgot Alexander at China Taste!* Then he remembered he wasn't on his own anymore; he lived with someone, someone who was watching Alexander while he picked up dinner.

Someone he was going to marry.

The whole thing had been his idea but he still

couldn't quite get used to it. He'd been solely responsible for his son and now Shelby would be equally responsible. As would he for Shane. That was the one
absolute they'd discussed so far in terms of how their
marriage would work. Shelby had brought up the idea
of setting parameters when she'd come up from Treasures an hour ago, and since they both needed to think
about what their must-haves and deal-breakers were,
they'd agreed that Liam would go pick up dinner and
they'd work it all out over lo mein and fried dumplings
and General Tso's chicken.

As he set the bag on the big coffee table, Shelby
hopped up and headed to the kitchen, and he could
barely take his eyes off her. She'd changed into faded
jeans that hugged her curves and long legs and wore a
V-neck dark blue ruffly shirt that made her eyes even
more emerald-like. She returned with a tray of plates,
silverware, glasses and a pitcher of iced tea. Both babies were fast asleep in the nursery, so the timing was
good for chowing down and having a very serious,
important discussion.

They dug in before getting to the nitty gritty of the
impending conversation. Liam tried to cut a dumpling
in half and it went flying across the coffee table, immediately inspected by her cat, Luna, who'd finally
warmed up to Liam. Luna wrinkled her nose at the
dumpling and walked away.

They shared a good laugh over that, the tension
abating somewhat.

"Ooh, vegetable fried rice—my favorite," she said,
heaping some on her plate.

"Mine, too."

"Well, ordering Chinese as a married couple will

be a snap," she said. "Except there may be arguments over leftovers."

"I'd always leave you the last dumpling," he said.

She tilted her head and looked at him. "You would, wouldn't you?"

He nodded. "I told you I'd never do anything to hurt you. That includes matters of the stomach."

She laughed. "Good to know." She ate a few more forkfuls. "So I guess we'd better start figuring out what we both expect from this marriage-to-be."

"Well, we have our first thing, that we are both equally responsible for both babies. That Shane is no more yours than mine. That Alexander is no more mine than yours. They are *our* children."

"Right. That's number one. It may take a little time, though, and we both need to be okay with it. I already love Alexander and I've known him for a weekend. I've loved Shane for his entire six months on earth and of course our bond is very strong. Both of us just need to catch up."

Liam nodded and twirled a forkful of lo mein. "Exactly. And we will."

"Number two," Shelby began, pushing around her fried rice as though stalling for time. "The marriage is legal, yes, but we'll have separate bedrooms."

The emphasis on the word *separate* told him she was talking about sex—the lack of, actually.

"Separate bedrooms, like now," he agreed. But the thought had been put in his head, about sharing a bedroom and lying next to soft, sweet, smart Shelby. She was so lovely, so sexy, without a shred of makeup and in jeans. He could so easily imagine lifting that ruffly shirt off her, seeing what was underneath. A lace bra. Underwear sexy just by virtue of it being on her luscious body.

His mind was going places it had no business wandering. Especially because he'd just agreed that their marriage would be platonic—which he'd always known would be the case. Separate bedrooms. No sex. No making out.

"Separate bedrooms," he agreed.

"Good," she said, forking a dumpling and dipping it in soy sauce.

"Right, good."

Good for the marriage, bad for him on a personal level because the control and restraint he'd have to put forth would zap all his energy.

Get back to the marriage—the reason for the marriage, he told himself. *Forget sex. You'll have to, anyway.*

"I have a condition, as well," he said, "One that goes in tandem with number one. Neither of us can make a decision about either baby without the other's agreement. I'm used to being the boss, so this won't be easy for me, but I know I don't want you to make decisions without my approval so I won't make any without yours."

"Agreed. I trust that we both have the babies' best interests at heart. After all, that's why we're getting married in the first place. So they both have the two of us. So we have the two of them."

Liam nodded. "So far, we make a great team. We see eye to eye."

"I know," she said. "It does make things easier."

They saw eye to eye because they were just plain compatible. They had the same values. They found the same things funny. And sad. They cared about the same things: two six-month-old boys. And those boys were the most important things in the world to both of them.

The marriage would work out fine. He was sure of it. If he could keep his attraction to Shelby at bay, the marriage would be a real success. There would be no hurt glances, no disappointments, no arguments over perceived romantic slights.

But keeping his emotional distance from her would be easier on his own turf. Here, everything *was* Shelby. It was all Shelby, all the time. At his ranch, there would be so much more space for the two of them. The four of them. It would be a hell of a lot easier to keep an emotional distance if he had a physical one.

And he'd need that, too. She was too close here, all the time.

He glanced around at her crowded apartment, then back at Shelby. "Is it important to you that we live here? I mean, it's cozy and I like being here, Shelby, but it's pretty small. I'd prefer we move out to my ranch. We can keep the boys together in the nursery, and you'll have a big bedroom. Plus, there's a family room and a lot of space for two boys to grow up."

"I'll make you a deal. We live here until they start walking. Then we'll move to the ranch since they'll need the space. But right now I need to be on my turf. Is that selfish? I know you probably feel the same way."

"I can understand, Shelby. You feel safe here. And your livelihood is downstairs. You're connected to your life here. We'll stay until they start walking."

He'd just deal with it. Power through. Try not to accidentally brush up against her in the small kitchen. Not imagine her naked in the shower in the one tiny bathroom.

Her smile lit up her entire face. But then it faded. "I've thought about the ceremony and all that. I decided on the Wedlock Creek Chapel, but maybe we should just go to the town hall and have Mayor Franklin marry us. After, we could throw a dinner party— at your ranch since this place couldn't hold one side of our families let alone both. Though my family will probably want to hold a part at the Pie Diner."

"Town hall? You sure that's what you want? Money is no object, Shelby. If you want a big wedding, I'm happy to give you the shindig of your dreams."

She put her fork down. "My dreams? Liam, the wedding of my dreams doesn't involve marrying a man I don't love. A man who doesn't love me. All the Mercer money can't change that."

"Understood," he said. "I just want this to be as... I don't even know. I'm asking a lot of you, Shelby. To—as you said, marry a man you don't love. I guess I just want to make it as easy as possible, to give you everything you want. Does that make sense?"

She smiled again. "Yes. And I appreciate it. But I come from a family of bakers, Liam, and we've known since birth that icing can't make a lopsided cake less lopsided."

"Well, then, let me tell you this. As your husband in this venture, Shelby, I'll always respect you in every way. You can count on me. Just know that. Maybe not in all the ways you used to think about. But you can count on me."

"It might take me a while to believe that, really

believe it. So don't take it personally if I don't seem to trust you right away. Given my past…" Her cheeks pinkened and she pushed more rice around on her plate.

"Shane's father hurt you pretty bad," he said gently, hating the idea of anyone hurting Shelby.

"Oh, just the usual case of saying one thing and then doing the complete opposite. He said all the right things, all the right romantic things, and I fell big-time. We got married after a whirlwind relationship. But just when I discovered I was pregnant, I found out he had two girlfriends. I confronted him and he said he was young and a free spirit and 'wasn't that why I fell for him?' Uh, no. He filed for divorce and left town with the one girlfriend he said he was his true love. When I was around six months along, I heard he died in a car accident."

"Sorry," he said. "It couldn't have been an easy time to be pregnant and treated that way."

"I never felt so alone. Or scared. I just kept thinking, what about the baby? He won't have a father? It wasn't supposed to be like this."

"Life can be like that, huh?"

She gave him something of a smile. "Don't we know it."

He reached for her hand and held it for a second. "I'll never betray you, Shelby. I can promise you that."

"Well, this isn't a love marriage, so betrayal really isn't an issue."

"There are lots of ways to betray someone."

She looked at him, her expression serious. "Yeah. You're right."

"But it's true that we're not in this for love or romance. This is about both of us having our children, becoming a family. It's about family."

She nodded.

He could keep telling himself this wasn't about romance all he wanted. But he couldn't take his eyes off Shelby. Couldn't stop picturing her naked. Couldn't stop imagining his hands gliding up her shirt, exploring every inch of her skin.

He wanted her, but he'd control himself, of course; control was Liam Mercer's middle name.

He took a sip of his beer. "Tomorrow, let's apply for our marriage license and find out what we need to do there, then we can start the ball rolling on formally adopting the boys. I'm not even sure if we each need to adopt the babies we took home. We'll need to get all our questions answered."

"This could have gone so differently if we were different people. Or if one of us or even both of us were married or involved with significant others. I think I should be grateful to have this opportunity to have both boys."

"That's how I look at it." He was grateful. And marrying to make it all happen wasn't taking anything away from him since he hadn't planned on marrying anyone. Loving anyone.

"After everything you went through with Shane's father, you still believe in love and happily-ever-after?" he asked.

"That's moot now," she said.

He wondered if she didn't answer because she did still believe in love or because she didn't. But she was right. The topic was moot. They'd marry to have their family unit.

This was a business partnership, really, with family as the business and the partnership. He was good at business. He'd be good at this marriage.

"So we each know what to expect, what this marriage will involve, and we'll be off to a great start," he said.

"My sister, Norah, texted me earlier. If we choose to get married at the Wedlock Creek Chapel, Annie and Abe Potterowski, the caretakers and officiants, can marry us on Wednesday at noon. There are no waiting periods or blood tests required in Wyoming."

"I hate the words *blood test*," Liam said.

She smiled. "Me, too. I hate it more than any words in the English language." She bit her lip. "You know what I also hate? The idea of marrying at the town hall. I love the Wedlock Creek Chapel, and since our marriage is going to be legal and binding, then we might as well have the ceremony in a beautiful, old chapel where I once—"

"Once what?" he asked.

She shook her head. "Doesn't matter. I'm set on the chapel."

He nodded. "Wednesday at noon, it is. Will you have your family there? I'm not sure about inviting my parents. My father and I are still on the outs. But I can't imagine getting married without my brother being there, no matter what kind of marriage it is."

"Let's have our families. Maybe it'll help your dad to understand why we're doing it, why it's so important."

"I don't even want to look at him," Liam said, turning away. He'd suddenly lost his appetite for the extra serving of General Tso's chicken he'd put on his plate.

"I'm not going to think about him. I'm not going to let him get to me again. He can feel how he wants. I'm my own man."

"You are. But he's your father and that word is powerful, as you know. He'll come to see why he's on the wrong side of this, Liam. But you may have to be patient with him."

"He doesn't deserve my patience. He deserves a kick. He deserves to never see me or Alexander—or Shane—again."

"Well, that'll hurt him, yes. But it'll hurt Alexander and Shane, too. And you."

"Can we change the subject?" he asked, handing her a fortune cookie.

"We can change the subject," she said, taking the cookie from the wrapper and snapping it in half. "My fortune says, learn by going where you have to go." She raised an eyebrow. "Uh, what?"

"I guess that's what you're doing. What we're both doing. We have to get married. We'll learn en route."

"Yes, but learn what?"

"How to make it work?" he suggested. "How to live with each other? How to be parents to children we've just met?"

"I'm putting this fortune in my wallet. I like it."

He smiled and cracked open his fortune cookie, pulling out the small slip of white paper. "Mine says, the best year-round temperature is a warm heart and a cool head. I've got the cool head, I think. Except when it comes to my father. Warm heart for my children. So I'm good, right?"

"I think it means to be passionate but practical. I like that one, too."

"Passionate and practical cancel each other out, though. Like our marriage. It's practical. It can't be passionate. Can you imagine what might happen if we let attraction into the picture?" He shook his head. "Whoa, boy."

"What would happen?" she asked, leaning forward.

"The minute you let romance in, there's a heart waiting to be broken. We can't risk that in our situation, Shelby. So no matter how much I may want to make love to you, I'll never so much as kiss you on the lips."

"You want to rip my clothes off?"

"You're a beautiful woman, Shelby. I'm just saying that I'm going to keep a certain distance. This marriage is to let us both have both babies. That's it."

"Right," she said. "The family unit."

He nodded. "You know, before I found out about Alexander and Shane, I was thinking about how much I wanted Alexander to have a mother. And how I was going to make that happen given that I didn't want to marry. At least that worked out."

She stared at him for a moment, then nodded slowly as if she was working out something in her mind. Surely she felt the same way after what she'd been through, no matter that she still believed in love. She wouldn't have to worry about heartache or loss and her baby—her babies—would have a father. A loving father who'd do anything for them and her.

How he was going to keep his mind off Shelby as a woman was going to take some doing, though.

Shelby turned over in bed and started at her alarm clock. 1:37 a.m. She'd been tossing and turning all night again, bits and pieces of Liam's words echoing in her head. *Want to make love to you... Going to keep my distance... For the sake of our children...*

On Wednesday she'd be marrying him. For good reason. So she had to put everything else out of her mind. Her plans, her former hopes, her future dreams. She should be grateful that Liam Mercer was a single, gorgeous, sexy, very kind and loving father. He could have been a total troll. So many could-have-beens would have derailed any hope of her having Shane and Alexander in her future. Now she wouldn't have any worries about that. *Thank your lucky stars*, she told herself, throwing off the blanket. She'd make herself a cup of herbal tea, the chamomile that always soothed her back to sleep, and wake up refreshed and ready to become Mrs. Mercer tomorrow.

She left her room, the apartment quiet. Liam's door was ajar, and for a half second she was tempted to poke her head in and watch him sleep. Maybe he'd be half-naked again. Instead, she headed to the kitchen and rummaged in the cupboard for the tea and sugar, then filled up the kettle and sat down at the kitchen table. Her gaze landed on the brown paper bag containing the music box—the other day she'd put the bag on top of the refrigerator and promptly forgot about it. No wonder, given everything going on in her life.

The secret note! She popped up and retrieved the bag and set it on the table, eager to see if anything was written on the folded-up piece of paper hidden under the lining. She might not be having a hot and passionate romance herself, but perhaps the secret note-writer had and penned a love letter he or she had never intended to send.

Careful to get to the boiling kettle before it could let out its whistle and wake up the whole apartment, Shelby poured her tea and waited for it to steep, then took out the music box.

Once again, she edged back the pink velvet lining and pulled out the folded piece of paper—plain white unlined stationery, a bit yellowed with age. It was a letter, written in neat black script. Her gaze went to the bottom of the page. It was signed *Mama*. It was to: *My dear son.*

And dated fifty-eight years ago.

Wow. Over half a century old. Given its age and that there were no names, Shelby felt justified in reading it.

My dear child,
You'll be coming into the world any day now. I know I won't be able to care for you properly— I can barely feed myself, let alone make sure a newborn has what he needs, especially for the upcoming winter. A drafty, depressing apartment above a bar is no place to raise a child. But that's all I can afford and I just don't see any way out.

Mrs. Mercer says you'll want for nothing and that you'll be so loved that you'll never know you weren't her own flesh and blood. When she said that, I admit I broke down and cried. But I know what she meant. She'll love you just as I would. And she can give you what you need, what you deserve, whereas you'd have a hardscrabble life with me. You'd be called a bastard your whole life. I want more for you, my precious baby. So

*you'll go with Mrs. Mercer the moment you're
born. You'll be her child. But know that I did
love you just as much and always will, forever.
    Mama*

Shelby stood up slowly, her legs shaky, and paced
the kitchen. What the hell? The letter was dated fifty-
eight years ago. Which meant the baby in question
was Liam's father?

She glanced at the name on the brown paper bag.
Harrington Mercer.

Someone had left the bag containing the music box
on Harrington Mercer's porch. Someone who knew
the letter was hidden under the lining and wanted him
to know the truth? Who? It would have been easy to
miss the hidden letter entirely. The Mercers had given
away the box without even knowing the letter was
there—that Shelby was sure of.

Perhaps the person who left it figured Larissa Mercer would open the package out of curiosity, open the
music box, see the uneven lining and edge it back to
find out what was underneath. But that was a risk.
After all, Larissa Mercer hadn't even gotten that far.

But Larissa had opened the package and unwrapped it. She'd even twisted the music prong to
see if it worked because she'd mentioned it played
one of her favorite sonatas. Perhaps whoever left it
on the Mercer doorstep knew Larissa would at least
open it? Maybe it was one of those *Well I'm going to
do my part by putting the box where it needs to be
and if the person meant to find the letter does, great.
If not, at least I tried.*

Maybe the person who left the box was the mother herself? Or a friend or relative of the mother?

Shelby read the letter again. What was the mother's connection to Mrs. Mercer? How had they even met, given the difference in their "stations," especially almost sixty years ago? And *was* "Mrs. Mercer" Liam's grandmother—Alexandra, whom Alexander was named for? Or a different Mrs. Mercer?

Question after question flew at Shelby.

The biggest one at the moment was whether or not she should wake up Liam to show him the letter. Surely it could wait until morning, not that she'd manage to get a wink of sleep now.

But considering that Liam was suddenly standing in the kitchen doorway, in those sexy sweats and a University of Wyoming Cowboys T-shirt, it looked like it was going to be now.

Chapter Nine

Liam had heard Shelby get out of bed because he'd been tossing and turning all night and his ears were trained on the nursery. But instead of hearing any middle-of-the-night cries from the babies, he'd heard Shelby get up and head to the kitchen. He'd thought about giving her privacy with her thoughts; he was sure it was the wedding—the entire idea of getting married—that kept her awake, but if he could ease her mind, he'd try.

"Couldn't sleep again?" he asked, coming in the kitchen and taking a mug from the cupboard. "Is there enough water in the kettle for another cup?"

She nodded. "I've been tossing and turning for so long I figured I might need a few cups to help me back to sleep."

He added a tea bag to the mug and poured the still-steaming water on it, then sat down next to Shelby. She held a letter, the old jewelry box his mother had given her beside her.

"Found something in the box?" he asked, adding cream to the tea.

"I did, Liam. A letter hidden away under the lining right in the main compartment."

"Hidden away? A secret letter?"

She nodded. "It's almost sixty years old."

"What does it say?"

She took a deep breath. "Liam, I think you'd better read it. There's a reason this music box was left on your parents' porch. Someone wanted your father to find the letter. Or at least have the music box where the letter was hidden."

"Huh? What does the letter have to do with my father?"

"I think it's *to* him," she said, handing it over.

Liam frowned and took the letter. It was signed Mama. Well, his mother didn't refer to herself that way, so he doubted this was from his mother. Or to his father.

My dear son, he read, saddened by the first paragraph, by a mother-to-be wanting the best for her child and having to give him up.

At the second paragraph, at the line *Mrs. Mercer says you'll want for nothing and that you'll be so loved that you'll never know you weren't her own flesh and blood*, Liam shot up out of the chair. He quickly read the rest, then his gaze focused on the date. The year his father was born.

"My father was adopted by Alexandra Mercer?" he

said, voicing his thoughts aloud. "He never told me. He never let on that he was adopted."

"Maybe he doesn't know," Shelby said gently.

He stared at her. "Jesus. Maybe he doesn't." His gaze fell on the music box. "This was in there?"

"Tucked under this lining," she said, pointing at the pink velvet and showing how it edged away from the corners and could be inched over.

"So the box was his birth mother's? And she left it on my parents' porch? On the chance my rich, snobby parents might want some old music box and find a hidden letter? That hardly sounds plausible."

Shelby sipped her tea. "I know. I've been running through possible scenarios and nothing quite makes sense. I have the feeling someone who'd been close to the birth mother put the box on your parents' porch. A relative or friend. Someone who knew the secret and thought, well, let me finally deliver this letter that never got sent and if Harrington Mercer finds it, great, and if not, I tried."

Liam sat back down. "Why not just knock on the door and hand him the letter and explain everything?"

"Good question. I really don't know. Maybe whoever left the box made a promise never to reveal the secret?"

"God Almighty. Well, what the hell am I supposed to do with this information? Show him the letter? He obviously doesn't know he was adopted. And I told you how he reacted to the DNA results. DNA means a little too much to my father. It would kill him to find out he wasn't—in his own words—a *real* Mercer."

"Maybe we could investigate a bit. Try to find out the backstory and history. There must be a connection between your grandmother and the birth mother. Clearly, they crossed paths and a baby was passed between them. I could do a little surreptitious questioning of some of my elderly customers who've lived their entire lives in Wedlock Creek."

Liam nodded, his head about to explode. "Go ahead. I've had about enough of family mysteries for one weekend."

"Seriously," she said, covering his hand, and he was glad she was here.

"Do you have a family album? If Alexandra Mercer was pregnant in the months before your father was born, maybe this isn't about her and your father at all."

"That's true," he said. "I was getting ahead of myself for no reason. This probably has nothing to do with my grandmother and father at all."

Wasn't that what he said about Alexander being switched at birth with Shane?

Early Tuesday morning, Shelby watched downtown Wedlock Creek disappear as Liam drove them out to the ranch lands just fifteen miles out of town. Liam wanted to check out his family photo albums that he had at his house before heading to the office for the day. His plan was to take both babies to the Mercer Industries day care, unless Shelby wanted to stick with business as usual and take Shane to work with her at Treasures. Or both babies. But Shelby had been excited for Shane to spend the day with Alexander at the day care where they'd be doted on, and besides, it would free her up to dig into the family mystery behind the letter she'd found in the music box.

They drove down a long gravel drive that managed

to reflect the Wyoming wilderness and be perfectly manicured in a rustic way. A half mile up was an open wrought-iron gate with a metal sign: The Double M.

"Double M for the two Mercers?" she asked.

He smiled. "I guess now I'll have to change the name to the Triple M." He glanced at her, eyebrow risen. "Quadruple M since you'll be a Mercer, too."

She stared at the sign at they passed it. She didn't feel like a Mercer, but then again, she wasn't one yet.

"Might be easier to stick with the Double M for old times' sake. Or just The Mercer Ranch."

"Probably," he said, pulling up in front of a beautiful white farmhouse with shiny black shutters and a barn-red door. There were acres of land as far as the eye could see and pastures and hedges but no cattle or horses. As Liam had said, this wasn't a working ranch.

"It's so beautiful out here," she said, getting out of the car and heading to the back seat to take out Shane.

Liam did the same with Alexander. "I've missed it, even though I've only been gone a couple of days. I sit out on the porch and just watch the land, the trees rustle in the breeze, and I can often figure out a problem."

Maybe she'd been hasty in insisting they live in her apartment—even until the babies turned into toddlers. Maybe they could both use all this fresh air and open space to think, to have room to breathe.

"Come on in," he said, taking Shane's carrier and easily handling both. He set Alexander's down and unlocked the door, then picked him back up and they headed in.

Shelby gasped. This was not what she was expecting at all. The entry led into a huge open space with floor-to-ceiling windows on the back wall. Exquisite rugs and leather couches made a living room around a massive stone fireplace, and across the room was a play area for a baby with floor mats and a walker and bouncer seat and everything a baby could want, just like Liam had said.

Huh. Shane sure would like that play area. And Shelby could imagine waking up here every morning, having this view with her morning coffee. Her mind would be clear until it focused on how her life had changed so dramatically so quickly. And then while she'd have a minor panic attack, she'd have the view and the natural beauty of this ranch to calm her down.

"I love it," she said. "Your home is beautiful."

"Wait till you see the room that would be yours," he said. "My cousin Clara decorated a guest room for me since the rest of the place is so masculine. I'll bet you'll like it."

She had no doubt she would. He carried the boys up the grand staircase to the second floor. He pointed out his room and a bit farther down the hall he opened a door. "This is the nursery."

She walked in and for the second time in five minutes, she gasped. "My God. This is a prince's nursery."

"Guilty," he said. "A little too much disposable income and loving the heck out of Alexander, and I ended up with this."

The crib was gold and she wouldn't be surprised if it was made out of twenty-four-karat gold. A mural of Winnie the Pooh with one of Shelby's favorite wise quotes from the sweet little bear was on one wall. A giant stuffed giraffe was in one corner, and one wall was lined with low, built-in bookcases full of board books and children's classics. A glider chair was by a window along with every type of baby paraphernalia imaginable. All the fanciest, the most expensive brands. The room was as grand a nursery as she'd ever seen.

"The nursery at your place is just as nice," he said. "It has everything they need—you were right about that. Fancy doesn't make the room better."

Tears poked at her eyes. "You know what I'm thinking about? The letter. How the birth mother wrote that she wanted more for her unborn baby than she knew she could provide."

He touched her shoulder. "Shelby, you're hardly destitute. I like your place just fine."

"I appreciate that. But even I wouldn't pass up the chance to live here. Alexander and Shane can be real Wyoming cowboys on this ranch."

"If you're sure," he said. "Why don't we move both of you in after the wedding?"

She nodded. "And either I'll take the boys with me to Treasures for the day or you'll take them to the day care. Maybe we'll split the week."

"Sounds good." He looked at her and reached for her hand. "We will make this work. I promise."

She nodded, needing to change the subject. She didn't want to talk about them, about their businessy marriage. "So where do you keep the family albums?"

"In the family room," he said. He picked up both carriers, and they went back downstairs. Liam set the babies in the gated play area, carefully babyproofed, she noted, and headed over to the wall of bookcases. He took out two leather albums and sat down on the brown leather sofa.

She sat beside him, eager to see a photograph of Alexandra Mercer—and if she'd been pregnant in the nine months before Harrington Mercer was born. "I hope there are pictures of her at the right time."

"There's an entire album devoted to her, my grandfather, Wilton, and my dad as a baby. I haven't looked in these albums in ages, but I'll bet there are lots of photos of her when she was expecting."

Except there weren't. Not one.

There were several photos of a nursery in various stages of development, so clearly Wilton and Alexandra had been expecting a baby. But as Liam flipped the pages of the album, there were no photos of her in the family way. One photo was dated January, nine months before his father was born. Alexandra Mercer was slim, her tummy washboard flat in a 1950s-style tucked-in sweater. The next photo was dated October, with Alexandra and Wilton holding infant Harrington. There were countless photos of Harrington as a newborn.

"Look!" Shelby said. "There's a photo of your grandparents leaving the hospital with your dad. Cottonwood County."

"So did she give birth there—or did the birth mother? And my grandparents brought my dad home."

The rest of the albums gave nothing away. They were all of Harrington Mercer growing up.

"Maybe there's another album of the nine months before your dad was born?" Shelby asked.

"Maybe. I only have these two. I'm sure my parents will have all the albums. They're not much into nostalgia but I'm sure they kept old photos."

"And you're all right with me doing a little careful poking into the memories of my elderly customers? The Minnow sisters were very involved in the town when they were younger and they've been in Wedlock Creek all their lives. Maybe they'll remember when your grandmother was pregnant. Or not pregnant."

"As long as you ask in a roundabout way. If my father was adopted and doesn't know, which I imagine he doesn't, I certainly don't want him and his story becoming gossip."

"I'll be careful, I promise. I trust the Minnow sisters."

He nodded. "Well, I'll show you around the rest of the house and property and then we'll both go to work. Like it's just a normal day." He laughed and shook his head. "As if there's anything normal about finding out on Friday that your baby was switched at birth, and then getting married on Wednesday to the mother of the baby he was switched with. And we can't leave out finding a secret half-century-old note about my father."

"It does feel good to go about our lives as normally as possible," she said. "Being at Treasures always makes me feel connected to myself. And I've been very at odds and ends this entire weekend."

He reached for her hand again. "I know. But hopefully once we're married and we're settled in here as a family, that'll become the new normal."

She smiled at his optimism. For someone who didn't believe in love or happy-ever-after, he sure was open to possibility. That was good.

But she couldn't imagine anything about any of this feeling remotely normal. Ever.

* * *

Shelby closed Treasures early for the day and met her sister, mother and Aunt Cheyenne at Finders Keepers, the one shop in Wedlock Creek that sold dresses.

"Um, Shelby, you can't get married in a denim jumper," Norah said, sliding dresses on the rack and shaking her head. "Oh, a turtleneck dress with long sleeves that goes to the ankles. Very bridal."

"I'm not really going for bridal," Shelby reminded her family.

"Sweetheart," her mother said, "you may not be going for bridal, but you are getting married. For real. Legally wed and all that." She paused in front of a pale pink dress. "How about something like this? It's pretty but not formal."

Shelby stared at the dress, which she did like. Very much, actually. It was silky and floaty. "I think I should wear something a little less pretty. More functional."

"Like this," Aunt Cheyenne said, handing Shelby a pale yellow sundress, simple and cotton with eyelet around the hem.

"That screams barbecue at the Mercer mansion. I'm thinking more...workish."

"This?" Norah asked, wrinkling her nose at how clearly plain and dull she found it.

Shelby smiled at the off-white, sleeveless shift dress. "Perfect."

Her relatives looked incredibly disappointed by the lack of adornment.

"At least wear amazing shoes," Norah said. "You'll have the photos forever."

"I have a pair of slingbacks that'll work," Shelby said. "Well, we're done."

"I hope you'll consider wearing Grandma's earrings," her mother said. "I wore them for my wedding and they brought me luck for over two decades."

Shelby could use some luck. "I'd love to. Thanks, Mom."

But the mention of her own grandmother reminded her of Liam's. Just what went on fifty-eight years ago between Alexandra Mercer and the woman who wrote the letter to Harrington? Who was the woman? How did they meet? And what happened to her? Shelby had so many questions and not a single answer.

"I'm closing the Pie Diner for a private party tomorrow from twelve-thirty to one-thirty."

"Oh?" Shelby asked. "What's the occasion?"

Her mother shook her head. "My daughter's getting married."

Shelby smiled. "Ah. That'll be nice, Mom."

"I'll leave it to you to invite the Mercers," her mom said. "We can meet and get to know one another at the party."

Shelby nodded. A casual wedding reception might be just the thing to bring Liam and his dad back together. She knew his father's attitude about Alexander had caused a rift between the men that both might be too stubborn to try to fix.

She thought about the letter, about the fact that Harrington Mercer was likely adopted and might not know it. Would finding out destroy him? If he couldn't handle his own grandson not being a "real Mercer," how could he ever accept not being one himself?

She was about to remind herself that this wasn't

her business and should butt out and let Liam handle it. But she was marrying into this family. And Alexander and Shane were forever tied to the Mercers. So it was her business.

And wasn't she about to be a Mercer herself?

Chapter Ten

On Wednesday morning, Liam set a jar of Alexander's favorite baby food, sweet potatoes, on the tray of his high chair, and a jar of Shane's favorite, apricots, on his, and did double duty, a spoonful to Alexander and a spoonful to Shane.

"Guess what, guys?" he said as both boys slurped around the spoons. "I'm marrying your mother today. We'll put you in your best sleeper outfits."

Shane stared at him with his big blue eyes. As Liam fed the baby another spoonful of apricots, he reached over and caressed Shane's cheek. The little guy wrapped his little hand around Liam's pointer finger.

"Bwabawa!" Shane gurgled, a big smile on his adorable face.

And just like that, something shifted inside Liam, a door opened a crack and love beams filtered through.

You're my son, Liam said silently to Shane, his heart about to burst. *We have a lot of lost time to make up for, don't we?*

At least I can feel it for babies, he thought, even if his heart was closed to romance. At least he wasn't a total goner.

"I'm your daddy," he whispered to Shane. "And I'm your daddy," he whispered to Alexander, spooning apricots into his open mouth.

"Bahababa!" Alexander babbled, picking up his toy key set and banging on the high chair.

His phone buzzed with a text. His cousin Clara.

We'll see you at the chapel at noon and then at the Pie Diner immediately following.

Did *we'll* include his father? Liam had called his parents yesterday to tell them about the wedding, and his mother had been surprised but happy and agreed it was a good solution. He'd heard his father grumbling about a prenup and Liam had sighed and told his mother the wedding plans and said a hasty goodbye.

He had no idea if his father would show up.

At least he knew the bride would be there. Last night Shelby had been quiet and had spent most of the night in her bedroom. Twice he'd knocked to see if she was okay and twice she said she was fine, just mentally preparing for a major event in her life.

He knew the impending marriage was keeping her up at night. Joining together as husband and wife solely to keep the family together. They'd make it work because they had to.

"I guess it's okay for you to see the bride before the ceremony in our case," Shelby said, coming into the kitchen. "Anyway, I'll be getting dressed at my mom's house and so I'll meet you over there. You'll bring the boys or should I take one with me?"

"I'll bring them both."

He watched her take a deep breath. "Well, I'll see you at noon, then."

"Shelby," he said as she was about to leave the kitchen.

She turned around.

"Everything's going to be okay. I know I keep saying that. But it really will be okay. Better than okay. It'll be great. We'll make sure of it."

She managed something of a smile. "I'm holding you to that."

He wouldn't let her down. He might not be able to give her everything she wanted, but he'd give her a solid family.

"Bababa," Alexander said, slapping his tray.

"Bababa," Shane repeated happily.

Shelby smiled. "They're holding you to it, too."

He thought of the gold bands in his pocket. A symbol of strength and forever and infinity, of their vows to stand by each other. Yesterday he'd called Shelby's sister, Norah, for Shelby's ring size and he'd picked up two matching rings he thought Shelby would like.

Making good on the promise was everything to him. He wanted nothing more than for Alexander and Shane to have their mother and father, for him and

Shelby to have both their babies. This way, everyone was happy.

Except *happy* wasn't how he'd describe the look on Shelby's face as she left.

His cell rang, and he was glad to avoid thinking too much about it.

His brother, Drake. "Sweating bullets?" he asked.

"Not in the slightest," Liam said. "Cool, calm and collected."

"Cut me a break, Liam. You're getting married. It's a big deal."

Liam put down the spoon and jar of apricots. "Shelby and I are getting married so that we can both keep our babies and have the ones we were denied. It's a partnership based on a fundamental need. Like most mergers."

Drake laughed. "You're more like Dad than you realize, big brother."

Liam frowned. "What is *that* supposed to mean?"

"It means that sometimes you need someone to kick you upside the head."

"About?" he asked. Drake, who had a steady stream of "women in his life," was hardly someone he'd take advice from on the subject of marriage. "I know what I'm doing, Drake."

"I'm just saying you might be in for a rude awakening."

"Again—about what?"

"About what marriage is really going to be like," Drake said. "It's not a business partnership. Shelby is a person. Shane is a mini person. You can't crunch them like numbers and make everything add up. Or not."

"And what makes you an expert on marriage?" Liam asked.

"I'm not. But I know you. You don't look at Shelby the way you look at acquisition reports."

"Acquisition reports aren't a beautiful woman."

"Exactly."

"Can I go now? I'm halfway through feeding my sons."

He froze, staring in wonder at Shane. At Alexander. His sons. Plural.

There was dead silence on the phone. "Jesus, Liam. You just said *sons*. You went from having one son to two in less than a week."

"I know. I think it was the first time I said that, actually. Sons. I have two sons now. And that's why I'm marrying Shelby. And it's going to be the best-run partnership I've ever formed."

"Well, I'd never miss your wedding. I'll see you at the chapel at noon."

Unsettled, Liam hit End Call and tried to focus on the happy babies in their high chairs. Liam offered Alexander a Toasty O but he flung it at his cheek. Shane threw his toy keys across the room.

Now *this*, he was familiar with. This, he knew how to handle.

How he actually felt about Shelby or getting married—really, deep down? That was something he didn't want to think too deeply about.

The Wedlock Creek Chapel was a beautiful white clapboard building that looked a bit like a wedding cake. Built in 1895, the Victorian chapel had scallops on the tiers and a bell at the top that almost looked like a heart. Shelby had been surprised that when she'd gone inside, her heart hadn't dropped; she hadn't been thinking about her first wedding in the chapel at all. Her mind was on Liam and Shane and Alexander.

She stood in front of the floor-length mirror in the "bridal" room, her stomach doing flip flops. Her mother and aunt had kindly given her space and left her alone with Norah, who always had a way of calming Shelby down.

"My God, is he gorgeous," Norah was saying, peeking out past the opaque curtain on the arched window on the door. "He's in his Sunday best."

"Really?" Shelby asked, coming over to the door to look through.

She sucked in a breath at the sight of Liam, so incredibly handsome and sexy in a dark blue suit and tie. Shane and Alexander were in their carriers, and if Shelby wasn't mistaken, they were wearing sleepers that looked like tuxedos.

"Those babies are too adorable," Norah said. "God, you're lucky. You're getting a gorgeous, rich husband and two babies. I know last weekend was rough, Shelby, but God, did it turn around."

"It's not exactly fun and games to marry a man for any reason other than love and wanting to spend the rest of your life with him," Shelby reminded her dreamy-eyed younger sister.

"I know. But if you need to marry a guy, you couldn't do better than Liam Mercer."

Shelby took one last look at her groom, hardly able to drag her gaze away from him.

"Okay, let me see you," Norah said, inspecting her from every angle. "Dress, perfect. Makeup almost nonexistent but the bride insisted. Grandma's earrings—stunning. Ancient off-white sling backs from the back of your closet, passable. All in all, Shelby Ingalls, you look absolutely beautiful."

Shelby looked in the mirror. The dress might not be lace or beaded or have a train, but it was just right for her noontime wedding. She wouldn't have expectations in this outfit, in these old shoes; and her grandmother's earrings, worn by her mom at her own wedding, would serve as a blessing from generations past. Shelby liked that.

There was a tap at the door. "If you're ready," Annie, the elderly officiant, said. "Oh, and Shelby, you look absolutely lovely."

Shelby smiled at Annie, who poked her head back out and shut the door. "Am I ready?" she asked her sister. "To marry someone I didn't know last Thursday?"

"You're ready to marry Shane's father. You're ready to be Alexander's mother. Right?"

"Absolutely."

"Then you're ready," Norah said, opening the door.

There was no bridal march, but there was a red carpet creating an aisle to her groom. And there were three Ingallses on the left and five Mercers on the right, all in the same row.

Shelby focused on the babies in their tuxedo-printed sleepers and they looked so cute and sweet that she couldn't help the smile bursting from inside her. But when she glanced at her groom, waiting by the mayor's side, her smile faded. From nerves.

She was marrying this man. He would be her husband. Not in every sense of the word, but he would be hers.

As she stood inches across from Liam, facing him, she forced the cotton from her ears and the strange sensation from her head to focus on the mayor's words.

"Do you, Shelby Rae Ingalls, take Liam West Mercer as your lawfully wedded husband?" Annie asked.

She looked at Liam, who was looking directly in her eyes, not a hint of worry or concern. *Because he's getting exactly what he wants and needs.* The family unit. A mother for Alexander. His biological child, Shane. An agreement: no love, no romance, no passion.

She glanced at the babies in their tuxedo sleepers. *You're doing this for them. And for you. So you can have them both without worry.*

And you're doing it for Liam, whom you've come to care deeply about.

Because he's a good man.

A thoughtful man.

A kind man.

"I do," she said.

Liam repeated his vows, and rings were slid on their fingers, hers fitting so perfectly that she knew her new husband must have involved her sister for her ring size.

Some plain gold band. The ring was beautiful, gold and studded with diamonds. It twinkled on her finger.

"You may now kiss the bride," Abe said, and Liam reached over and gave her a quick peck on the lips.

"Congratulations, Mr. and Mrs. Mercer!" Annie and her husband, Abe, shouted.

The audience stood and clapped.

Shelby noticed that Liam's father took a minute to get himself up, as though he barely thought it necessary. The man was angry and upset in a place deep inside, Shelby could tell. Liam's mother looked a bit confused, as though she didn't understand how she'd gotten here, at her son's wedding to a woman she'd never heard of before last weekend. Liam's brother, who'd announced that he was the best man in spirit if not practice, clapped Liam on the back and shook his hand then hugged Shelby and welcomed her to the family.

"It's not like this is a real marriage," Harrington Mercer said. "You two only got married because of the situation you found yourselves in."

"If real and legal are synonyms when it comes to weddings, then this is real," Liam said, a slight growl in his voice.

His father turned away, and Larissa Mercer frowned in commiseration with her son and new daughter-in-law and said, "We'll see you at the Pie Diner."

Liam's cousin Clara and Shelby's family jumped in front of the newlyweds with their phones, snapping photos, so there was no time for Liam to react to his father's dismissal.

"Guys, pick up the babies," Norah said. "We need a few shots of you holding your children."

That was what this was all about, Shelby thought, scooping up Alexander while Liam picked up Shane.

She gasped. "This is the first time I associated the words *your children* with Alexander," she said, tears coming to her eyes. "Normally I'd go for Shane. But I went straight for Alexander." She snuggled him against her chest. "You're my son and you always will be. Just like Shane."

Liam kissed Shane's forehead. "Switch for more pictures?"

They switched. The familiarity of Shane in her arms was comforting. Now she'd have all the time in the world for Alexander to feel as familiar. She held him close, taking in every bit of his sweet little face, the tiny dimple in his right cheek, his inquisitive blue eyes and quirking bow mouth.

"What a shot," Aunt Cheyenne said, showing her phone to her sister and niece. "I'm going to have this one printed out and framed for you, Shel."

Her family must have taken a hundred shots of them in the boring old room and more outside. Some folks passing by gawked—the gossip mill would be running once word got out that the second-hand shop owner had married a mighty Mercer.

"Oh, Shelby and Liam," Annie said, her blue eyes misty with tears as she linked her arm around Abe's. "I'm so happy for both of you! And just think, the Wedlock Creek legend has already come true for you!"

Shelby glanced at her brand-new husband. "Um, Annie, I'm not pregnant. With one, two, or three babies."

"Yeah, but you have twins now, don't you?" Abe said, straightening his blue bow tie. "Those little fellas are exactly the same age, born the same day at practically the same time. They're as close to twins as you get without being blood related."

Shelby gasped.

Liam raised an eyebrow.

"Well, we definitely have multiples," Shelby said, looking down at Shane and Alexander. "There are indeed two of them."

Liam tilted his head. "Huh. Multiples." He smiled and gave each baby a gentle caress on the head. "I did get married in the chapel and I do have multiples." He looked at Annie. "How does that legend go? Multiples in some, way, shape or form?"

"Yup," Annie said. "I can add another notch to the wall of couples for whom the legend came true."

While Shelby tried not to think about the legend coming three-quarters true and what that might mean, they all made their way to the Pie Diner, which Shelby's family had decorated with Congratulations banner and balloons and streamers.

The Mercers, including Harrington, were warm and friendly and everyone enjoyed the pie sampling, coffee and iced tea. But when Harrington asked to hold Shane and made a special point to bond with the little boy, Shelby couldn't help but notice Liam watching his father. Watching his father *not* hold Alexander—even once. Watching his father not look Alexander's way.

All the other Mercers treated Alexander as the adored grandson he'd always been and they fussed over Shane as the new addition to the family. But Harrington never veered from his focus on Shane.

God. The man clearly didn't know he'd been adopted. Because if he did know, DNA couldn't possibly mean so much to him. He'd know that family was a word built on love and commitment and taking responsibility and caring.

As Shelby listened to Clara Mercer rave to Norah about how amazing the chocolate chip peanut butter pie was, she glanced over at Liam, who was staring at his father, eyes narrowed, as Harrington Mercer held Shane and pointed out the window at a little red bird on a tree.

Shelby knew her new husband enough by now to

know that he was steaming mad and that there was going to be a showdown. Maybe not today—not on their wedding day, however practicality-focused it was. But a showdown was coming. And truth be told, Shelby had a feeling Liam would learn a thing or two about how love really worked, too. Because you couldn't pick and choose whom you loved. If you were capable of the emotion, and Liam clearly was, you couldn't just decide you weren't going to love the woman you had to marry. Just like his father couldn't decide he suddenly didn't love his six-month-old grandson because he wasn't a "real Mercer."

If Liam couldn't love her it was because chemistry and the mysterious properties of love just worked that way. But to decide you weren't going to love? Nope, didn't work that way.

And Shelby knew both men were going to find that out the hard way.

Because Liam felt something more than just friendship. That was one of the few things she was absolutely sure of. She looked down at her beautiful wedding ring sparkling on her left hand. Yes, she was sure.

There were surprises waiting for Shelby at her new home. She knew she'd be moving in after the wedding and had packed two suitcases to start, but Liam had not only moved all the babies' things into the nursery at the ranch, he'd also added another fancy crib for Shane and had his name painted on the wall above with the U of Wyoming Cowboys' logo beside it.

Liam had been right when he'd said Shelby would love the guest room his cousin Clara had decorated. The moment she stepped in she felt like she was at the beach, in a bungalow designed just for her, with the most soothing of pale blues and yellows and white, a hint of pink here and there. There was a glider chair by the window by a bin of baby paraphernalia, everything she could need to soothe a fussy little one in the middle of the night.

There were red roses in a vase on her bedside table.

A plush white robe and matching slippers on the edge of the bed.

And a big wrapped gift on the bed itself.

"What's this?" she asked, suddenly feeling a little too aware of the bed in the room. On her wedding night. Well, wedding late afternoon. But still. A bed. A wedding ring. A husband and wife. And nothing was going to happen.

"A gift for you," he said.

Shelby smiled at the huge gift. It was rectangular and she had no idea what it could be. She took off the giant silver bow, then ripped open the wrapping paper.

"Oh, Liam," she said, staring at it. "This is absolutely beautiful."

It was a treasure chest, a hope chest, antique white with her name stenciled across the top in gold. She had a few hope chests for sale in her shop and they always went quickly, but she'd never found one that she wanted herself—until now. She loved it.

"I've always wanted one. Thank you, Liam."

"I have a big desk drawer where I keep all Alexander's keepsakes. I figured a hope chest would be nicer. More room as the boys grow up."

She bit her lip, a little too verklempt to speak. "It's perfect. I have something for you, too."

She dug in her tote bag on her shoulder for the wrapped box and then handed it to him.

He unwrapped it and smiled. It was a photo of Alexander and Shane in their bouncers, and Shelby had caught a moment when Shane was reaching toward Alexander's little cowboy hat. Shelby put it in a pretty antique frame she'd found at an estate sale.

"That little cowboy hat makes me very sad now, unfortunately," he said.

Oh, darn. She hadn't even thought of that when she'd wrapped the gift this morning. She thought it so well represented who Alexander was, who Liam was.

He stared at the picture. "Well, if my father is really the baby in that letter you found in the music box, we know one thing for sure. He doesn't know he was adopted. Or he'd never turn his back on Alexander just because they're not blood relations."

"I was thinking the same thing at the Pie Diner. I'm so sorry, Liam."

"How do you just stop loving a six-month-old baby? It's insane."

She nodded. "There's no way he stopped loving Alexander. He's just put a wall up. That's all. And walls can be blasted through."

"Walls are strong, though. And my father is stubborn."

"Talk to him. Tell him how you feel. Tell him how painful this is—not just for you but for Alexander. He might be little now, but to be rejected by his own grandfather?"

"The hell he will reject him!" Liam shouted. "I won't stand for it. I'll give him a couple of weeks to come around. After that, if he doesn't, well, there won't be any more Mercer family Fridays."

"You can't cut him out of your life."

"Why not? If he cuts Alexander from his?"

"God, this is complicated."

"No, it's not, Shelby. Love and family aren't complicated when it comes right down to it. Take us, for example. We went into this knowing exactly what's what, right? It's not like I was madly in love with you and then upended the status quo or changed the rules midway because of this or that."

"But you're so sure you can't change your mind about love, Liam."

Had she said that aloud? She felt her cheeks burn a bit, hating that she'd exposed herself. But maybe she had to. For both their sakes. If he was going to help his father, maybe she had to help him see how stubborn *he* was being.

"Not *can't*. The way I feel about romantic love is a decision. To opt out."

"And what if you fall madly in love with me, Liam? How are you going to opt out?"

"I'm not going to fall in love with you. Because I've made a decision not to."

She smiled. "Right. Because that's how romantic love works. Liam, please. Romantic love conks you over the head."

"I can choose not to—that's all I'm saying. And I do choose that. Because I've experienced the devastation firsthand—twice. And I'm not going through that again. Now I have everything I want and need. My two sons. A mother who loves them both. And nothing will come between us—because we're not romantically involved. We're a partnership."

She took a deep breath. "Liam, your dad is choosing not to love Alexander right now. That's not okay with you."

He sat down on the edge of the bed. "I'm not so sure it's a choice. I mean, I don't think he woke up and decided that Alexander isn't his grandson. It's a feeling that came over him very strongly out of... fear, I guess."

"Choice, not a choice. We can go around and around trying to figure all this out. Your father will come around. I believe that."

"You have more faith than I do."

"I know," she said. "Believe me."

He stared at her then, and his blue eyes narrowed, but he didn't ask what she meant—or what she was really talking about. Because he probably didn't want to delve too deeply into his own feelings about love and romance and marriage.

She had a good seventeen and a half years ahead of her to help Liam Mercer open his heart to her. She wondered what would happen after the boys' high school graduations. When they turned eighteen and were legal adults. Would Liam say, "Well, we did our jobs and now we can go our separate ways?"

She had no idea. The subject had never come up and was so far in the future there was no point. Shelby wasn't so sure she could see a month into the future, what it was going to feel like to wake up every day as this man's wife. But not his *real* wife in the true sense of the word.

Suddenly, real and not real were more complicated than she expected.

"So," he said. "This is a special occasion. How about I make us two great steaks and we have some wine?"

That sounded kind of romantic. And like a good start, even if he didn't intend it that way.

Chapter Eleven

Liam woke up the day after his wedding, the photograph of Alexander and Shane on his bedside table the first thing he saw.

The second thing: his wedding band.

Liam had taken the rest of the week off to research what they needed to do about adopting the boys, to investigate the letter in the music box and most important, to bond individually with the switched baby and to spend time together as a family.

Liam had made breakfast for everyone, blueberry pancakes for him and Shelby, and boy, had she been surprised that he cooked—and pretty well, too. Then they packed up and headed to the Wedlock Creek park. April in Wyoming wasn't exactly short sleeves weather but the sun was bright and they walked the path along the river and showed the babies the beauty of Wyoming wilderness.

A visit to the courthouse in the county seat informed them that the magistrate had no idea about the legalities and ins and outs of their situation but would make calls. Shelby and Liam let the man know they'd like to formally petition to adopt both boys so that there was no question as to their legal status as the boys' parents.

That taken care of, they had a picnic lunch on the town green, thankful that a taco truck had taken up residence in the center of Wedlock Creek. Otherwise, there was only a coffee shop, an Italian restaurant where everyone celebrated special occasions and a saloon-like steakhouse with amazing mashed potatoes and creamed spinach.

After sort of crawling on the big picnic blanket for a little while, both babies managed to tucker themselves out and were now fast asleep in their carriers. Liam held up his soda can. "A toast to our first full day as a family unit. Went great, I'd say."

She clinked colas with him. "I agree. This marriage may be a practical partnership, but today felt truly special, Liam. Thank you."

And then she leaned close and kissed his cheek. A sweet kiss. A thank-you. Nothing more.

But desire and instinct had taken over and before he could stop himself, he put both hands on either side of her face and kissed her full on the lips.

He pulled back and blinked. Why had he done that? "Whoa. Swept away by the moment. Sorry about that."

"I'm not, Liam. Swept away is a good thing. It's natural. It's—"

"It's not going to happen again. Don't you worry."

He'd make sure of it. For the sake of the two little guys napping inches away, he couldn't fall in love with their mother. Because falling in love led to eventual discord and disappointment and broken hearts. Right now things were close to perfect. They were becoming true friends, real friends. Last night, over steak and his garlic mashed potatoes and wine, they'd sat on the couch in the living room, talking about everything from the time Shelby climbed a tree in her front yard and couldn't get down and the fire department from two towns over had to come get her out, to when Liam was named President of Mercer Industries, what he'd thought was the happiest day of his life.

Until Alexander was placed in his arms by a doctor at the clinic, the same doctor who'd had him sit down for the news about Liza.

He couldn't quite call that the happiest day; not with losing Liza, with Alexander never having the chance to know his lovely mother. But it had been the most special, the most moving—the first time he held his son, his child. The first time he felt the fierce love of parenthood.

They'd talked for hours, moving between serious memories to lighthearted ones. And they talked about the babies—Shelby had filled him in on everything he'd missed in Shane's six months on earth. The ear infection from hell. The first time she heard him laugh. The way she could have the worst day of her life and then look at Shane, needing everything she didn't have left to give, but finding it because she loved him so much.

He knew exactly what she meant.

And then she'd reached for her wineglass and her sweater lifted enough for him to see an expanse of creamy soft skin at her waist and between that and the curve of her breasts and her beautiful profile and sexy hair, he was overcome with lust.

More than lust. Last night he hadn't just wanted to have sex with Shelby. He'd wanted to make love to her. Slowly and lovingly and for hours.

And so he'd retreated, missing her the moment they'd said their good-nights and their bedroom doors closed.

He had to be careful. And it wasn't just now. Kissing her like that, being spontaneous, doing what he felt like doing instead of being his usual guarded self.

Being spontaneous and doing what he felt like sure felt better than holding back all the time.

"Penny for your thoughts," she said. "A dime for inflation."

"I'm just glad we're in this together," he said. Again—spontaneously. Couldn't he have told her he wanted another turkey sandwich?

"Me, too," she said, squeezing his hand.

And he didn't want to let go.

The next morning, as Shelby turned the sign on the door of Treasures to Open, one of her favorite customers, Charlotte Linden, came in, a small cardboard box in her arms.

"Charlotte, let me help you," Shelby said, rushing over.

"Oh, please," Charlotte said. "I might be seventy-eight but guess who just came from hot yoga? And I kept up with the millennials, too."

Shelby smiled. "No doubt." Charlotte was glowing with good health. "Just trying to be a doting proprietor. What do you have for me?"

Charlotte opened the box. "I inherited these from my great-aunt years ago and to be honest, I think they're the ugliest things I've seen. I don't like frogs, though. Some people do."

Shelby laughed. Two matching miniature lamps with a bronze frog inlaid on the base. "You know who loves frogs? Callie Minnow. I'll bet she'll grab them the moment I put them on display. I'll give you fifteen for the pair."

"Twenty and we have a deal."

She'd list them for twenty-five and break even at twenty when Callie, as expected, would fall in love with them this Friday.

"Oh, my goodness!" Charlotte exclaimed suddenly, her mouth hanging open. "Is that what I think it is?"

Charlotte was staring at the ring on Shelby's left hand. Shelby had just started getting used to the feel of it. But every time the beautiful, sparkling diamonds caught her eye she would stop and wonder: Where did this come from? I'm married? When did that happen? She was always taken by surprise. Maybe that would go away in time. When being married—and to Liam—felt like…real life.

"Sure is. I got married yesterday. To Liam Mercer."

Charlotte's eyes widened. "Liam Mercer? You're kidding. You gonna sell this place?"

"Now, why would I do that? I love Treasures. I love when someone just like you comes in with frog lamps to sell and I know just who will want to buy them."

"You're a millionaire now. You don't have to work."

A millionaire. Shelby Ingalls? She almost laughed. Then realized it was sort of true. Liam had told her he would not ask her to sign a prenuptial agreement because no matter what, their relationship would be forever. "Regardless of my new husband's net worth, Treasures is my heart, Charlotte. You know that."

"Those Mercers like things their way. Trust me, I know that family going way back. You'll have to stand your ground. I hope you will."

The hairs rose on the back of Shelby's neck—and not because Charlotte sounded at all mildly foreboding. The part about "knowing the family from way back" meant she might have information about Wilton and Alexandra Mercer. "Oh, I will. I don't think Liam would have it any other way." *Ask her about the Mercer family*, she told herself. *This is your opening.* "So, Charlotte, you knew Liam's grandparents? Wilton and Alexandra?"

"Well, of course I knew them. Knew of them, really. Like everyone in Wedlock Creek in some fashion or another. They had glittering parties every weekend at their fancy ranch. If you were invited, you knew you'd arrived." She smirked. "I was never invited, of course. Oh, the beautiful dresses and coats Alexandra Mercer used to wear—even to the park and to pick up milk at the store. She was so glamorous. She was really the first businesswoman many of us in town ever knew of. Some say she was the serious brains behind Mercer Industries. I admired her, I must say."

Shelby smiled. "Did she keep working while she was pregnant?" Shelby practically held her breath, waiting for what information Charlotte might have.

"Hmm, I really don't know. Like I said, I only really knew of her and saw her around town sometimes. But I did see her once when she was heavily pregnant. She looked so happy. I remember thinking, now there's a baby who'll have everything he or she ever dreamed of."

Heavily pregnant. So Liam's father wasn't adopted? Then what was the letter in the music box about? Based on the year the letter was dated, Harrington Mercer was the baby in question.

"Must be nice to be so rich," Charlotte said. "And now you know, too, my dear." Before Shelby could tell Charlotte that she had no intention of living her life any differently than she always had, Charlotte added, "My friend Pearl used to work for the Mercers as a maid and was responsible for caring for the jewelry. She told me the first time she saw the collection she almost fainted from shock."

As a maid. The words echoed in Shelby's mind. Maids had a way of seeing and hearing things because they were often considered invisible. Maybe Pearl could share some of her memories of Alexandra and Wilton—and the pregnancy.

"I'd love to meet Pearl and hear about those old times," Shelby said. "Liam was young when Alexandra died, and he said his parents don't talk much about themselves or the family."

Charlotte smiled. "Of course you're interested! Because you appreciate the past and all its history and stories. It's no wonder you own a secondhand shop. You know that big old farmhouse off the service road? That's Pearl's. She has a dog rescue. You'll hear the dogs barking and you'll know you're close."

"Thanks, Charlotte. I'll stop by tomorrow."

Shelby couldn't wait to tell Liam about the lead. And she had a feeling they were about to uncover a big Mercer family mystery.

On Saturday morning, with Norah filling in for Shelby at Treasures for the morning and her mother and aunt Cheyenne babysitting "the multiples" as Norah had taken to calling them, Shelby and Liam headed to Pearl's farmhouse. Just as Charlotte had said, they heard the dogs barking and a curve in the road led right to the house. Six dogs, all sweet mutts, ran up to the car, excited to see who'd come to visit.

"Let the poor folks have a path, for goodness' sake," a woman said as she came down the porch steps from the house. She appeared to be in her early eighties. She was tall and looked strong and robust, a long, silver braid tossed over one shoulder, green mud boots on her feet. "Are you here to adopt six dogs? They're yours." She smiled and laughed, and Shelby could hear the affection in her voice for the dogs.

"Actually, with two babies and a skittish cat, we're not looking for a dog," Shelby said. "A friend, Charlotte Linden, told me you worked as a maid for the Mercer family years ago. I was hoping you could tell us about your time with the family."

"Interesting timing," Pearl said, eyeing Liam.

"Meaning?" he asked, glancing at Shelby.

"You're Liam Mercer, right?" Pearl looked him over from head to toe and back up again.

"I am," Liam said. "Interesting timing because our visit is either a total coincidence or you left the music box on my parents' porch?"

Shelby almost held her breath. Had she?

Pearl lifted her chin. "I'm sure it's no coincidence. I did leave the music box on their porch. But I'm surprised Harrington Mercer isn't here himself to ask questions. I suppose he sent you to try to find the person who wrote the letter."

Shelby and Liam stared at each other for a moment. Thank you, Charlotte! The woman and her frog lamps had led them right to the very woman who'd left the jewelry box for Liam's father. "Actually, Harrington never saw the letter," Shelby said. "His wife found the package on the doorstep, thought the box was lovely, but said their house was overflowing with stuff and she donated it to my shop, Treasures. I found the letter under the lining while examining the box."

"Ah. So Harrington never saw the letter," Pearl said, and it was hard for Shelby to tell how the woman felt about it. She seemed to be thinking about it, considering it. But her expression gave nothing away.

Liam shook his head. "Not yet, anyway." He stared at Pearl. "Charlotte told Shelby that she recalled seeing my grandmother, Alexandra, when she was heavily pregnant. So we're confused. If Alexandra was pregnant and gave birth to my father, then…"

"She wasn't pregnant," Pearl said. "She didn't give birth to your father."

What? "But—"

"I'll get to that," Pearl said. "It's quite a story. Anyway, anyone can look pregnant with the right device or pillow strategically placed. Actresses wear that kind of stuff for movies all the time."

Liam stared at Pearl, taking that bit in. "Are you my father's birth mother?"

"Goodness, no," Pearl said. "But I know who was. I was her friend."

Was, Shelby thought, tucking that away for now.

"So it's true," Liam said, surprise and wonder in his voice. "My father was adopted by Alexandra and Wilton Mercer?"

Pearl nodded. "Yes. At birth." She glanced at Liam and bit her lip. "Why don't I make some coffee and we'll talk."

Liam nodded. "Thank you," he added, strain in his voice.

"Well, come on in, then," Pearl said. "Make yourselves comfortable," she added, leading the way into the living room and gesturing at the couch and love seat and overstuffed chairs.

As Pearl disappeared into another room, Shelby squeezed Liam's hand and sat down beside a cocker spaniel napping on the couch. The dog eyed Shelby, gave her a sniff, then went back to sleep. Liam finally sat down beside her, hands on his hips as if bracing himself for what was to come.

"I didn't doubt the letter," he whispered. "But to hear it said so plainly…to learn something so fundamental about my father all these years later…" He shook his head.

"Something he likely doesn't know about himself," Shelby said.

Liam nodded and turned away. They'd had their share of major surprises concerning close relatives— that was for sure.

Pearl returned with a tray holding a silver coffeepot and three cups and cream and sugar. She sat down on the love seat across from them and poured three cups.

Liam fixed his and then sat back. "What was it like working for my grandparents?"

"They treated me well," Pearl said. "I even got myself promoted to head maid. They were good to me."

"Pearl," Liam said, taking a sip of his coffee. "How did you come into possession of the letter to my father?"

Pearl took a sip of her own coffee. The cocker spaniel jumped off the couch and jumped up next to Pearl, curled next to her and went back to sleep. "I had a good friend named Jeannie. She wasn't in the best of health and it was hard for her to work, but she was all alone in the world and had to earn a living, so I got her a job on the housekeeping staff at the Mercer mansion. Your grandmother employed a housekeeper who had three maids reporting to her."

A housekeeper and three maids—one being the head maid. Shelby couldn't imagine. At that point, Alexandra and Wilton were childless, too.

"Well, poor Jeannie put her hopes in the wrong man who turned out to be a cad. He got her pregnant and that was the last she ever saw of him. Jeannie could barely take care of herself and was so scared about her future—her child's future."

Shelby's heart squeezed. Shelby had done the same—trusted the wrong guy. But at least she'd had family support. She'd never been on her own, not really.

"I feel so sorry for her," Liam said. "To be all alone like that."

Pearl nodded. "We were all struggling, but Jeannie's poor health added to her problems. Well, one day she had terrible morning sickness and had to sit down and chose to sit right on Alexandra Mercer's new divan the moment Mrs. Mercer was coming down the stairs. Your grandmother did not look pleased. But by then, Jeannie was beginning to show and your grandmother's expression changed. Mrs. Mercer took Jeannie into another room."

"Now things are beginning to make sense," Liam said.

Shelby nodded. "Did Jeannie tell you what was discussed?"

"It took some prodding but she finally did. She swore me to secrecy because Mrs. Mercer swore her to secrecy. Jeannie told me that Mrs. Mercer asked if she was in trouble, and when Jeannie told her she was, that the baby's father had abandoned her, that she was sickly, and had no idea what to do, Mrs. Mercer offered to adopt the baby and give Jeannie enough money to convalesce out of town. Far away from Wedlock Creek. Jeannie said that Mrs. Mercer promised to raise the baby with all the love in her heart and that the little one would want for nothing."

"What a position to be in," Liam said, shaking his head.

Pearl nodded. "Jeannie was both relieved and heartbroken. She knew letting her boss adopt her child was the best thing for the baby. And so she followed Mrs. Mercer's instructions to the letter. Mrs. Mercer rented her a small home a few towns over, paid for her prenatal care, and when the baby came, took the newborn son home to Mercer mansion. No one knew the child had been adopted. It was all a big secret."

"And no one was the wiser because my grandmother wore a prosthetic of some kind," Liam noted.

"Exactly," Pearl said. "One that grew as needed with the passing months. No one knew. I'm sure her husband did, of course. But no one else. Your grandmother didn't like the ruse, though, so she kept a very low profile for almost the entirety pregnancy."

"Wow," Liam said, seemingly speechless.

Shelby leaned forward. "Pearl, what happened to Jeannie?"

"She died a few months after the baby was born. Complications from a flu strain or something like that, the doctor had said. In the weeks before she died, she gave me the music box, the one thing she'd never sold for money, and said she'd tucked a letter under the lining for her baby boy, that maybe one day, if the time was ever right, it would find its way to him. I wasn't sure I wanted the responsibility of deciding when the right time was."

"I can understand that," Shelby said.

"A closed adoption, a secret adoption at that," Liam said. "Sharing that letter would affect many lives."

"Right," Pearl said. "Which was why I held on to it for almost sixty years. But now that I'm in my eighties... I don't know. It just seemed wrong to hold something so...vital, a truth that does matter, that does mean something. It felt wrong to take it to my grave."

"So you put it in a bag with Harrington's name on it and left it on his porch," Liam said.

Pearl nodded. "I figured one of two things would happen. It would be brought to Harrington Mercer and he would take a look, notice the bumpy lining and see what was tucked under and find the letter. Or, a maid or his wife would find the package, mention it to him, get dismissed and toss the box in the garbage or the attic. I just wanted to try—to do something that might get the letter to him, exactly as it had been given to me. I admit, I hadn't considered the music box might end up in Treasures, a secondhand shop where someone else might find the letter. In fact, I figured no one ever would."

Shelby took a sip of her coffee. "But someone did. And not just someone—Harrington Mercer's son's new wife."

Pearl seemed to notice Shelby's ring for the first time. She gasped. "Congratulations!" she exclaimed. "Isn't that something? I thought by leaving that box on the porch that whatever would be would be. But perhaps it ended up in just the right hands after all."

"Why is that?" Liam asked.

"Because you're family," Pearl said gently. "You'll know whether you should reveal the secret or burn the letter."

Liam let out a breath. "God, I don't want that responsibility."

"I know just how you feel," Pearl said. "Sorry."

Shelby took the last sip of her coffee. "Pearl, do you think it's possible that Harrington Mercer knows he was adopted?"

Pearl shook her head. "I can't see how. Alexandra went as far as to fake her pregnancy. She swore Jeannie to secrecy."

"Do you think I should tell my father?" Liam asked Pearl.

"That's for you to decide," Pearl said. "It all comes down to whether or not you think he would benefit in any way from the information, whether it would change his life in a positive way. If it would only hurt, then no, maybe not. I'm just not sure, dear. Truth is important, but then ignorance is bliss. Right?"

Shelby thought about Shane and Alexander. She'd been living in ignorant bliss for six months while the baby she'd given birth to was being raised by someone else, also living in ignorant bliss.

"I really don't know," Liam said. "Not anymore."

And with that, they thanked Pearl for everything they'd shared, said goodbye to the dogs who'd come to see them off, and then left, both of them quiet on the ride home.

Her new husband had quite a decision to make.

Chapter Twelve

Liam sure was glad to be back home at the ranch and not at Shelby's tiny apartment. He'd walked the fields for over an hour, Shane against his chest in a sling. Shelby had taken Alexander to work with her, wanting to show him the shop and point out all her favorite pieces.

And Liam had pointed out all his favorite spots on the ranch to Shane. Starting with the outdoor play yard his father had ordered as a surprise for Alexander to celebrate his one month on earth. There was a big cedar playground with swings and slide and a jungle gym for when he was a bit older, and a toddler area with pint-size climbers and hidey spots.

"You and Alexander will play here together as brothers," Liam said, one hand against the protective sling at Shane's back, the other on the wood fence surrounding the play yard.

Shane looked at him with those beautiful blue eyes.

"One day, when the time is right, Shane, I'll tell you about your birth mother. Liza was a wonderful person. And I know she's looking out for you and always will be watching over you."

Shane's little bow mouth quirked. Liam caressed his soft cheek, so in love with this precious boy that he felt like his heart would burst. "I lost the first six months of your life but I want you to know I'll always be here for you. No matter what," he added. "You're my son. Same as Alexander."

If only his dad could see it that way. That Alexander was Liam's son same as Shane. How could the man who'd raised him have such a different way of looking at things? How could they have such different values?

"DNA alone doesn't make you family," Liam said, watching a bird land on a post. "Family is about love and taking responsibility and commitment."

How could his father not understand that?

And because Harrington Mercer didn't understand that, how could Liam show him the letter Shelby had found in that music box?

But how could Liam *not*?

"I've been walking around that question for over an hour, Shane," Liam said, heading back toward the house. "And I'm no closer to knowing what I'm going to do than I was when your mother and I left Pearl's house."

"Ba-la!" Shane babbled, reaching out a hand.

Liam smiled and shook Shane's tiny hand. "What should I do, wise one?"

"Ba-wa!" Shane said with a huge smile.

Unfortunately, Liam could take that to mean anything: tell him or don't tell him.

Maybe Shelby would have some advice. "Let's go home and wait for your mother. If I know Shelby Ingalls—Shelby *Mercer*," he corrected, "she'll have been thinking about it all day at work. It's good to surround yourself with smart women, Shane. Remember that."

On the way to the house, he'd decided he should share the letter with his father.

But by the time he opened the door, he'd changed his mind.

That went on for a good hour more until Shelby finally came home with Alexander. The sight of them made him forget all about the questions buzzing at his brain. Shelby, as usual, looked so beautiful, her blond hair loose around her shoulders, her V-neck sweater bringing out the green in her eyes.

"Make any decisions today?" Shelby asked, shifting Alexander in her arms.

He slapped a hand against his forehead. "I just put it out of my mind a second ago after killing myself all afternoon."

She smiled. "Sorry. We don't have to talk about it. You don't have to decide anything right away."

"Except it feels awful, knowing a secret about someone—and not just someone, my father."

"Let's put these two to bed and then I'll make us comfort food for dinner and we'll talk it out."

"Sounds like a plan," Liam said.

Comfort food. Smart woman talking him through this. Just what the doctor ordered. They headed upstairs to the nursery bathroom, took care of baths, fresh pajamas, two stories, three songs and many kisses good-night. Both boys stirred and fussed a bit before finally falling asleep, but finally, Liam heard nothing but Shelby's cat, which had taken up residence at his ranch, meowing for her dinner.

"How about you feed Lulu while I take care of dinner," Shelby said with a smile.

Liam knew he had the easier job and gave the cat her can of ocean fish in gravy. "Can I help?" he asked Shelby.

"You can take this and yourself into the living room and relax," she said, handing him a beer.

"You're good to me," he said.

"You're good to me."

The marriage was a success. Plain and simple. Granted, they'd been married since Tuesday, but it was working. They *were* good to each other. Good for each other. And good for Alexander and Shane.

Liam sat down on the couch, put his feet up on the coffee table, and enjoyed his beer, trying to not think too much about whether or not he was going to tell his father about the letter. Every time he thought he made the right choice, he'd change his mind.

"Dinner is served," Shelby said, coming in with a tray that she set on the coffee table. "My favorite comfort food. And I'm going to admit that I didn't make it. It's Norah's special tonight at the Pie Diner. Beef pot pie."

"It smells amazing," he said, sniffing the air. His mouth was already watering for it.

She cut him a big slice, succulent beef stew, soft chunks of potatoes, carrots and who knew what else making for a great-smelling dinner. He took a bite—

delicious. "Please tell Norah this is the best pot pie I've ever had."

She smiled. "I will."

"What do you think I should do?" he asked. "About the letter?"

"What I think is that you know your father best. I did agree with what Pearl said, that sharing the letter with him may be the right choice if it would benefit him. But I was thinking about how everyone involved has passed on," she pointed out. "His parents. Jeannie. He'd have Pearl for information, but the three people he'd really want to talk to about it are gone."

He hadn't considered that. "That's a good point."

Shelby took a bite of her pot pie. "What she said about Jeannie really touched me. How alone she was. It made me think about how lucky I am to have my family. I can always count on them. And for your father, he has a loving family, too. He has your mother, you, your brother. So if you did decide to share the letter, he wouldn't be alone. He may not be able to turn to his parents or Jeannie for answers or clarification, but he'd have you guys."

"Another good point."

She smiled. "Not very helpful, I know."

Liam sipped his beer. "I've been trying to think about how telling him would help him see that DNA isn't the be all and end all. That not having Mercer DNA doesn't make him less of a Mercer. I'm still a Mercer, right? If I am, then Alexander is. Same as Shane. None of us is more Mercer than another. Especially given the new information we have about my father."

"Except he feels how he feels. The news might devastate him."

"Except it shouldn't. He's still the same person he was. That's what he needs to understand. Which makes me think I should tell him."

"You'll do the right thing," she said. "That's all I really know for sure."

"I appreciate your faith in me. Believe me. Sometimes I have zero in myself."

She reached over and kissed him on the cheek and again, he took her face in his hands and kissed her.

But this time, she kissed him back.

Which made pulling away impossible.

He couldn't if he wanted to. And he didn't want to. He wanted Shelby in his arms. His hands were suddenly everywhere, in her hair and under her sweater, moving to her waist and rib cage and her breasts, hidden by something lacy. He kissed her hard, leaning her back on the couch, and she wrapped her arms around him, her husky breaths and little moans pushing him toward the edge.

She shifted slightly. "Liam, not to be a cliché, but I don't want to do anything you're going to regret."

"What?" he asked, kissing her neck.

"Right now you're caught up in the moment. You're turned on. You're not thinking. And when you do start thinking, like after we've had sex, when we're spooned together and you're suddenly itchy and uncomfortable and realizing you messed up your perfect vision of our family unit partnership. You'll pull away, I'll get hurt and guess what—the discord you were afraid of from the start."

He reached up a hand to her face, to her soft cheek

in a gesture of thanks. *She cares about me, for real*, he realized.

And that was scary enough to make him sit up.

"You're absolutely right," he said. "Thank God one of us is always on their toes."

She moved a few inches away on the couch, clasping her hands in her lap. "I need to be careful with you, Liam. Very careful."

"Meaning?"

"Meaning we're obviously physically attracted to each other. We're married. We share a home, a family, a crazy situation that brought us very close. If I give in to how I'm feeling, my inhibitions loosened with a glass of wine, I could end up losing everything that matters to me. You know, I used to think you were being too cautious. But now, who knows what would happen if we hated each other's guts? If we were fighting for custody. And for whom?"

His stomach churned. *But I want you so bad*, he thought. *You're one hundred percent right, yet how am I going to keep my hands off you? You're all I think about now.*

"Let's eat," she said. "And watch the news. That's always good for killing the mood."

As she pointed the remote at the big-screen TV, Liam sighed inwardly and picked up his plate. Hadn't he told Shane how important it was to surround yourself with smart women? Shelby was being smart. A hell of a lot smarter than Liam had acted a minute ago.

But he wasn't supposed to want her with this kind of ferocity. He wasn't supposed to fall in love with her.

His own wife.

* * *

Fool, Shelby chastised herself as she tossed and turned in bed—alone. Yes, she believed every word of what she'd said to stop him, to stop *them*, from getting into trouble, from doing anything that could jeopardize their very good arrangement. Their *marriage*.

Sometimes when Shelby thought about the way they were both keeping one giant step back from each other—emotionally, physically—the whole idea seemed so dopey. *Just kiss and make love and go from there, idiots!* she wanted to yell at them sometimes. And if it turned out that Liam was hot for her physically but thought she was a snooze otherwise? Then what? They'd be "friends with benefits" but married? Or what if they made love and she realized she just didn't feel "that way" about him? He'd be hurt and suddenly there would be cold shoulders and distance and who would pay? Two six-month-olds, that was who.

Not worth the cost. Being with Liam, truly being with him, was priceless. But losing her babies? She wouldn't jeopardize having both of them in her life every day, living with them as a family. She couldn't.

So great. She and Liam were on the same page. To cold showers and wishing things could be different.

She flipped onto her stomach. Then on her back. Then to her side. Her other side. Dammit! She couldn't get comfortable. She wasn't comfortable.

Because she already loved her husband. And was just not acting on that love. She knew Liam cared about her, but she wouldn't say he *loved* her. Wanted her, maybe. Okay, definitely. He'd proved that tonight. But a man as passionate as Liam Mercer wouldn't be able to control himself to the degree he had so far if he loved her. Hadn't he said over and over that what he wanted most was for the four of them to be a family unit? He was a red-blooded male, he was attracted to her and he'd acted on that a time or two. Didn't mean he was in love.

So get your head out of the clouds, Shelby.

And get out of bed, she told herself. She might as well go check on the babies.

She put on the fancy spa bathrobe that Liam had provided her in her en-suite bath, then padded down the hall. A soft light glowed from the nursery. The night-lights?

She pushed open the door. Liam was fast asleep in the glider by the window, *Moo Baa, La, La, La* open on his lap. Once again, he was shirtless. In sweatpants. Barefoot. And so sexy she could hardly take it.

Sexy because he was hot, hot, hot.

Sexy because he was kind.

Sexy because he was a great father.

Sexy because he was a good husband.

How much longer could they really go on this way? Both afraid of getting hurt. Both afraid of destroying the family? Both afraid of losing Shane and Alexander. Was this what they wanted to teach their children? To avoid real life and real emotion and how messy the heart could get?

Shelby sighed and headed back to her room. Tomorrow, Liam would tell his father about the letter—or not. She had a feeling that doing so, or not doing so, would change *him* forever.

But in what way?

Chapter Thirteen

In the morning, with ten minutes to go until opening time, Shelby held Alexander against her chest and showed him the new collection of paintings that had been donated to the shop from a regular customer who'd inherited them from her grandmother and hated them all. Shelby liked quite a few of them and knew they'd sell, and the drearier still lifes might appeal to someone.

"What do you think, Alexander? I love the way the artist used a hint of pink to brighten up the gray sea in the background. And do you see the rowboat? I'd love to take you and Shane out on a rowboat when you're older and—"

A wheeze suddenly came out of Alexander's tiny body, a raspy cough that froze Shelby. And was it her imagination or was Alexander's face suddenly flushed—and mottled? He fussed and squirmed, and she put her hand to his forehead. Hot. Very hot. He coughed, wheezed again and Shelby's heartbeat sped up.

"Oh, no. You definitely have a high fever." She dashed upstairs to her apartment, where the nursery was still intact. She took Alexander's temperature. Scarily high. Grabbing her cell phone, she called the pediatrician, the same one she used for Shane, and was told to take him to the clinic right away and that he'd meet her there. She called Liam and explained the situation.

"Wheezing?" Liam repeated. "Like a cough from a cold? A high fever? That'll go down with some baby Tylenol, right? I mean, it's nothing, right?"

"Well, a fever that high can be alarming in babies, so Dr. Lewis just wants to examine him, make sure he doesn't need fluids—just double-check everything is okay."

"I'll meet you at the clinic in ten minutes. Shane's in the day care, well taken care of."

"Perfect," she said. "See you soon."

In less than ten minutes, Shelby was at the clinic. Dr. Lewis arrived quickly after and led the way into an examining room. Just as his stethoscope was going into his ears, a nurse led Liam into the room. He looked very worried.

He reached for her hand and held it, and again Shelby was struck by how real a couple they seemed, acted like—were, except for that one major area. Regardless, she sure was glad he was here.

"Well," Dr. Lewis said, "from the fever, wheezing and listening to his chest, it's clear he has RSV—

respiratory syncytial virus—a common childhood illness that often first strikes before two years of age."

"Is it serious?" Liam asked.

"It's serious, not life-threatening—no worries there. He has a touch of bronchiolitis, which means we'll need to watch his airways. He'll need to stay at the clinic for a few days so we can monitor him around the clock and also because he'll be contagious for at least a week."

"A week? But Alexander and Shane share a nursery at the ranch. There's a guest room we can move Alexander into when he's discharged."

"I don't think the two babies should share a home for at least a week," Dr. Lewis said. "Just to be safe. RSV is highly contagious."

"I'll keep Alexander at the apartment," Shelby suggested. "Shane can stay at the ranch with you. That way we can be sure Alexander will be fully cured before he comes back to the ranch. Shane will have less chance of catching RSV that way."

"I think that's the way to go," Dr. Lewis said.

Separated.

Just like they didn't want.

"It's just for a week," Liam said, his hand on Shelby's arm. "A week is nothing. We're in this for a lifetime."

She nodded and actually did feel better. In the grand scheme of things, a week was nothing. But every hour of every day would crawl by. She was glad to see Alexander through his illness, but she hated the idea of being away from Shane for so long. And Liam.

"I'll call my family and let them know what's going on. Expect pie deliveries," she said, mustering a smile.

"Pie always helps."

"Call your dad," she said. "One word about Alexander being sick and stuck in the clinic for days and he'll rush over with a life-size stuffed bull."

Liam frowned. "Bull being the key word, unfortunately. I'm sure he won't. Alexander isn't his *real* grandson, remember?"

"Liam, a baby in the hospital has a way of knocking through very stubborn walls. Call him."

"I'll call," he said. "But I'm not expecting his feelings to suddenly change."

Shelby sure hoped she was right about his dad. If she wasn't, it was the Mercer family that might never recover.

Liam delegated the afternoon's work to his cousin Clara, who promised to visit Alexander in the clinic when she left the office, and then he headed over to his parents' house with Shane. Shelby was right. She had to be right. His father would have a complete meltdown over his beloved Alexander being so sick and in the clinic for a few days. Liam figured he should tell his parents in person so that he and his father could begin mending their relationship right away. He didn't need problems with his father to burn in his gut when he was worried sick over his son.

His mother wasn't home, but his father was in his home office, having a glass of scotch and reading dossiers on companies that Mercer Industries might look into acquiring.

"There he is, my young man," Harrington Mercer said, his gaze on Shane in Liam's arms. He stood up and came around his deck, smiling at the baby. "Let me have my grandson."

Liam froze. The split second was long enough for his father to pluck Shane out of his grip and hoist him high in the air.

"Aren't you a magnificent young man," Harrington said. "We have a lot of catching up to do. I was just looking at companies that MI might buy. Here, come see."

He took Shane back around his desk and sat down, the baby gurgling happily on his lap. "Winston Tech had a terrible quarter. And honestly, I don't think their products are top-notch. Let's move on to Branston Manufacturing—"

"Dad," Liam said. "There's something you should know. Alexander is sick. He has RSV and it grew into bronchiolitis. He'll be at the Wedlock Creek Clinic for around three days, and then he'll stay with Shelby at her apartment while I keep Shane at the ranch to make sure Shane doesn't catch it."

"Well, that's smart," Harrington said. "Trust me, Shane, you don't want to catch some nasty virus. You'd miss a ton. Every day you soak up countless bits of knowledge and—"

Liam frowned. He waited a beat. His father continued chatting to Shane about osmosis and paying attention and how when he was three and started preschool, Harrington would add a home-school business segment to his curriculum. "Are you going to ask if Alexander is going to be okay?" Liam practically growled.

"I'm sure he is," Harrington said.

"He's going to be at the clinic for *days*, Dad."

"And he'll be fine when he's released."

A hot burst of anger, bordering on rage, bubbled in Liam's chest. "Jesus, you really don't care, do you?"

"Liam, for God's sake, stop overreacting. Alexander is no longer my grandson and you know it. He's an Ingalls. His people run the Pie Diner. This," he said, hoisting up Shane again, "is my grandson. And I need to focus on getting to know him."

Liam stormed around the desk and grabbed Shane away from his father. Shane stared at him, his little face crumpling. He rocked the baby a bit and patted his back. "Sorry, little guy. It's okay. Everything is okay."

But it wasn't. Not by a longshot.

"Goodbye, then," Liam said. "You don't know the meaning of family." He turned to leave, prepared to estrange himself from his father until the man woke up, which might never happen.

His father stood up. "Liam."

He turned, his stomach twisting. Harrington's expression was one Liam didn't often see. It looked to him like resignation.

"DNA matters," his father said. "Whether you like it or not."

He should just come out with it, tell his father what he'd learned about his own DNA, show him the letter, introduce him to Pearl. But to what end? To hurt him because Liam was hurt?

Tell him if there'll be some benefit, Pearl had said.

Would there be? If DNA mattered that much to his father, the truth about himself would destroy him. That wasn't what Liam wanted, either.

He might not like his father right now. Might not agree with him. Might not share his values.

But he loved his father and always would.

"I should know," Harrington said, his voice cracking. "Trust me. I *do* know."

Liam stared at his father, taking a step toward him. "Dad?"

Harrington walked to the wall of windows, his arms around himself protectively. He stood there looking out, inhaling, exhaling. "I know because I was adopted as a baby." He turned toward Liam and looked at him, then away. "Because I'm not a real Mercer."

Holy hell. He knew. He knew he was adopted.

"I can tell from your expression that you're shocked," Harrington said. "Of course, I couldn't tell you because then you might not think you were a real Mercer. I kept the secret to protect you."

Oh, Dad. Liam closed his eyes for a moment, letting this all sink in.

"I overheard an argument between my parents when I was nine," Harrington said. "I'd left for school but forgot a book and had come back. My parents were in the living room, their voices raised. I hid behind the wall and listened. My father said it was getting ridiculous that I didn't know, that he wasn't going to put up with it a day longer, but my mother pleaded with him to let it go, to just make it go away. At first I had no idea what they were talking about. But then I understood. I'd been adopted as a baby. My mother wanted my father to pretend that wasn't the case. That I was my parents' child, end of story."

Liam tried to picture his father, tall, strong, imposing Harrington Mercer, hiding in the kitchen and eavesdropping on an unbearable argument between his parents only to discover he'd been adopted. That a secret had been kept, a secret about him. Liam recalled photos of his father while looking for pictures of Alexandra Mercer during her pregnancy. He'd been a solemn-faced kid, with serious blue eyes. Liam could hardly bear imagining that boy standing there in shock, confused, hurt.

"My father kept saying that the truth was the truth and it was wrong to keep something so important from me, that I should know for many reasons. But then my mother said something I'll never forget. She said, 'It's too late. If he'd grown up knowing that would be different. But it's too late. It'll break his heart to know he's not a real Mercer.'"

"Oh, God. Dad." Tears pricked the backs of Liam's eyes and he blinked them away.

"I turned and ran then. I don't know what else was said. But I do know they never did tell me. Long after my mother died, when my father was in hospice and I'd visit him, he would hold my hand and tell me to never forget that I was a Mercer, that it would carry me through."

Liam's heart clenched. There was so much he didn't know about his dad. There was so much the people closest to you didn't reveal. Incidents and memories and trauma that seeped their way inside their bones, changing them this way or that.

"I never let on that I knew. I didn't want to break his heart at the end. And I know it would hurt him deeply to know that I'd known the truth for decades." He turned back to the windows, his chin lifted, the strain in his jawline evident. "But do you want to know what kept going through my mind as my father drifted in and out of consciousness? That I *wasn't* a real Mercer. That a lie *wouldn't* carry me through. To fill my father's shoes at Mercer Industries, I'd have to work very hard, make my life the business and try to become a Mercer in all the ways I knew how. I think I passed just fine. But I never felt like I truly belonged, that the name wasn't really mine."

Liam tried to process everything he'd just heard, but the words echoed in his head. *The name wasn't really mine.* "Given all you just said, how could you say that Alexander isn't a real Mercer, then? How could you turn your back? Your parents brought you up to be their son. That made you a Mercer. Not your DNA, Dad."

"Because the truth was unbearable, Liam. And Alexander is going to grow up knowing the truth. He's not a Mercer. He's an Ingalls. And I'm not going to lie and pretend he's something he's not. He's not my grandson. Shane is."

"So you're not a Mercer. That means I'm not. And guess what—that means Shane isn't, either. So it looks like you don't have *any* grandsons."

His father stared at him then, hard, then looked away.

"When does it end, Dad? Who gets to be a Mercer in this branch of the family?"

His father walked over to the bar and topped off his scotch. He didn't say anything.

"I have something for you, Dad. It's in the car. I'll be right back."

Liam's legs—and heart—felt so heavy as he walked out of the room. Part of him didn't want to leave his father alone with his thoughts, with the admission hanging in the air like that. But he wanted to give his father the music box and letter. The time had presented itself.

Liam returned to the room with the box, his father still standing by the windows. "Dad, do you remember Mom showing this to you? She found it in a brown paper bag with your name on it, left anonymously on the porch last week."

Harrington shrugged. "Your mother shows me a lot of things."

"Well, Mom gave it to Shelby for her secondhand shop, Treasures. But when Shelby saw the box, she fell in love with it and decided to keep it instead of offering it for sale. She was examining it and found a letter hidden away under the velvet inside lining."

"And?" his father asked, bored and impatient. He sipped his scotch and sat down in the club chair by the fireplace.

"Here," Liam said, handing him the box. "The letter is inside. You need to read it."

Harrington rolled his eyes but took the box. He opened it and unfolded the letter, his expression changing a second later as he read the date.

"That's my birthday. The day and year I was born," Harrington said, looking up for a moment and then returning his gaze to the letter.

Liam sat down on the chair across from his father, looking down, wanting to give the man some privacy.

He heard his father gasp and looked up. Liam knew exactly where he was in the letter. The first time "Mrs. Mercer" was mentioned.

Harrington sat still as a post, staring at the letter. He appeared to be rereading it, then again. His hands flew up to cover his eyes, his shoulders trembling.

His father was crying.

Liam got up and walked over to his father and

put his hand on his shoulder. Harrington stood and wrapped his arms around Liam, sobbing, and Liam held him tightly, saying nothing, just letting him cry it out. It was the third time he'd seen his father cry; the first time had been when Liam was just a kid, when his father's mother was dying, the second time at the funeral.

Harrington pulled back, wiping at his eyes. "Good God, this almost ended up in some stranger's house on the mantel."

Liam smiled. "But it didn't. It ended up in your daughter-in-law's hands. Shelby. Shelby *Mercer*. She's a Mercer because she married me. I'm a Mercer because you're my father. Alexander is a Mercer because I'm *his* father. And you're a Mercer because you're Wilton and Alexandra Mercer's son."

Tears glistened in Harrington's eyes. "I'm also this woman's son. Whoever she was."

"Yes. Also. Just like Shane is *also* my son. Even though I didn't raise him for the past six months. Even though someone else did. In that case, DNA says so. In Alexander's it's because I love him. *Love*, Dad. That's what matters. Your birth mother clearly loved you. Your adoptive parents clearly loved you. Love makes you family. Period."

Harrington stood up and moved to the windows again. Not saying a word.

"Shelby and I did a little investigating. It led us to a woman named Pearl who runs a dog rescue out of her home on the outskirts of town. Pearl is the one who left the letter. Your birth mother was her friend. She can tell you the story, if you want to hear it."

"I'm not sure," Harrington said, taking a sip of his drink.

"When you're ready, then," Liam said. "If you're ready." He walked over to his father and put his arm around him, then kissed his cheek, ignoring the way Harrington stiffened. *Tough nuggies*, Dad. In the doorway, he paused and turned around. "Oh, and Dad, I'll be at Alexander's bedside at the clinic till five and then I'll go pick up Shane and take him back to the ranch. Just to keep you in the loop."

His father nodded and again didn't say anything.

Liam had no idea where things would go from here. He just knew he was desperate to see Alexander and hear that he was improving, even though Shelby had told him exactly that an hour ago. But first he'd have to stop at the office and take care of some pressing business, then pick up Shane and drop him off at the Pie Diner with the Ingallses for the couple of hours he'd be at the clinic for visiting hours.

Liam wished he could just head over there right now. If he didn't see Shelby's face soon, hear her voice, feel her in his arms for a bracing hug, he would spontaneously combust.

"It's so hard to see a baby in the hospital," Norah said, barely able to hold the stuffed monkey, the five board books and the blanket with the chew ends she'd bought for Alexander. She glanced down at the little guy asleep in the bassinet.

"You're a sweetheart for bringing him all these presents," Shelby said. "Between you, Aunt Cheyenne, Mom, Liam's brother, mother and his cousin bringing heaps of gifts, we could open a big-box store."

Norah smiled. "Alexander's color looks pretty good."

Shelby nodded. "The doctor said he responded well to treatment. He may only have to stay here for two days."

One day less without Shane and Liam, the four of them together as a family. That was good. And so was the news that Alexander was already on the mend with antibiotics for the bronchiolitis and fluids.

Norah had to get back to the Pie Diner for the after-dinner rush, but just as she was leaving, Liam arrived. He hugged his sister-in-law, thanked her for all the pie she'd had delivered to his home and office, told her how her beef pot pie was the best he ever had and then turned to look at the stacks of gifts for Alexander.

"Wow. Alexander sure is loved."

And lucky. Like his cousin had said the morning Liam's entire life had turned upside down. Lucky because he was cherished.

"My parents came with the huge stuffed dolphin?" he asked, eyeing it in the corner.

"Actually, that was your brother's doing. The dolphin, the Harry Potter and Narnia collections on the windowsill and an iPod preprogrammed with lullabies by his favorite artists."

Liam smiled. "That's Drake, all right."

"And your mother brought that," she said, pointing to the giant play mat with all kinds of pop-up fun for a six-month-old. "She was very concerned about Alexander and said she'd call later to see how he was doing."

Liam frowned. "My father wasn't with her?"

Shelby shook her head. "He hasn't been here."

"How did my mother seem when she was here?"

"Uncomfortable. Upset."

"No doubt." Liam filled Shelby in on everything that had happened during his talk with his father.

"He's known he was adopted since he was nine years old," Shelby repeated, shaking her head. "That must have been so hard to process."

"What *isn't* hard to process? Loving a six-month-old baby. You don't get to pick and choose which baby to love."

Shelby reached out for Liam's hand. He was spitting mad, his cheeks flushed, his blue eyes flashing. She'd never seen him so angry.

"He should have been here. Two hours have passed since I left him. How could he not have rushed over here to see his grandson? How the hell can he act like this?" His voice was raised and he expelled a breath, looking in Alexander's bassinet to make sure he hadn't woken him. He closed his eyes for a moment and turned away, his arms crossed over his chest.

"Liam—"

He paced the room. "Just goes to show you how family can cut you to the quick. How you can't really let yourself count on anyone. What we're doing, Shelby, this arranged marriage with our list of dos and don'ts—that's how you set up a family. That way, no one gets hurt."

No, no, no, Shelby thought, her heart pleading. *We're supposed to move past this. The way we feel about each other is supposed to blast through this ridiculous arrangement and make our marriage real in every sense of the word.*

"Like I said," he continued, "you were right to stop

things last night. Thank God you did. Because all it would lead to is heartache. And I've had enough."

"No, Liam. I wasn't right."

He stared at her, waiting.

She stepped closer. "I was scared! Just like you are. But avoiding real love, a real marriage, because of fear—Liam, *that's* wrong."

He turned away and ran a hand through his hair. He was clearly frustrated and she could tell he was thinking she just didn't get it, didn't understand.

No, it's you who doesn't understand! Think about what you can have!

Yes, just explain that, she told herself. What was waiting for them if only he'd open that locked-up heart, guarded by bitter old trolls.

"Liam, every minute of our lives is going to be filled with risk. Alexander got sick. It could have been worse. It wasn't. Shane will fall out of a tree when he's five. Alexander will take a hard fall off a bike when he's eight. There will be accidents and mishaps and heartache and who knows what else. That's life. And we have to deal with it."

"Yes, stuff happens, Shelby. Believe me, I know. So do you. So let's not add to it by messing up a platonic marriage that's working just fine."

"You call this argument *fine*? You call going to bed every night alone *fine*? You call wishing we were truly together *fine*?" She paused, wondering if she was going too far. Maybe it was only she who felt this way. Her heart clenched as she realized Liam might not have the same depth of feeling for her. But everything inside her told her he did. "And what about the boys? Do you really want them to grow up thinking that a marriage is based on nothing more than practicality and friendship?"

He turned away again, let out a heavy sigh and faced her. "Nothing wrong with practicality and friendship. I'd say there are worse things to build a marriage on. Like nothing more than passion."

But we have it all! We have the friendship. We have the practicality. And we definitely have the passion!

She opened her mouth to say so, but he shook his head. "There's nothing more to say, Shelby. I'm going to pick up Shane and bring him home to the ranch. A few days apart will probably serve us well, anyway. Let you bond more with Alexander and me with Shane. And give us some time to forget last night ever happened and start fresh."

I don't want to start fresh. I love you! I want my husband in every sense of the word.

But now wasn't the time to make her case for that whopper. Liam was hurt and angry and lashing out. Maybe a little time to themselves was in order.

Maybe he'd come to his senses.

Except what if he didn't? Like father, like son?

A chill ran up Shelby's spine.

Liam stood by Alexander's crib and touched a kiss to his forehead, then left the room, taking Shelby's heart with him.

Chapter Fourteen

Alexander had been discharged the next afternoon, and Shelby brought him back to the apartment above her shop. Liam had called at least ten times for updates.

And to ask if his father had stopped by the clinic to see Alexander before he was sent home.

The answer was no, and the silence on the end of the phone made it clear that Liam hadn't made peace with his father's rejection overnight. As if that was possible, anyway.

Shelby had stayed at the clinic last night, watching Alexander's chest rising and falling with every breath, her love for him keeping her awake. She hadn't wanted to miss a moment. Not when she'd missed so much already. She must have fallen asleep eventually on the uncomfortable built-in "parent" cot, grooves in the side of her face, her hair a disaster and her back all wonky. Her mother had come by the clinic with sesame-seed bagels and cream cheese and orange juice and coffee and given Shelby a wonderful massage, and it had taken all Shelby's doing not to let loose with everything that had happened.

She usually would, but this was her husband's family business and it didn't feel right to blab about it just so she could feel better.

Except that was what family was for.

By the time Shelby was back home and Norah arrived a half hour before she had to open Treasures and take over as proprietor for the day, Shelby had let it all out.

"Oh, Shelby," Norah said, pouring them both coffee at the table in the kitchen. "He'll come around. The man loves you. The man is *in* love with you. He can't put the kibosh on that no matter how hard he tries."

Shelby felt her shoulder slump and dumped a teaspoon of sugar in her coffee. "His father did it."

"Baloney. His father is processing. The man was handed two big kicks upside the head—first that his grandson was switched at birth. Then that his birth mother left him a letter. He had a minute to process that letter yesterday when Liam expected him at the clinic. Give him a little time."

"That's a good point. Liam worries he's a lost cause."

Norah took a sip of her coffee, frowning at the pink-red lip gloss stain she left on the mug. "Look, I don't know Harrington Mercer. I barely talked to the man at your pie-diner wedding reception other than about his favorite kinds of pie. But I know people. And the man has heart."

Norah was awfully good at reading people. She always had been.

"You think so?" Shelby asked, feeling herself brighten a bit.

"I do. Oh, by the way—the lawyer and I broke up."

"Oh, no," Shelby said. David Dirk had been very good to Shelby during one of the most difficult days of her life. "You okay? Here I've been hogging the conversation and you have your own big news."

"Big schmig. And it's not big at all. I'm totally fine. He told me he met the woman of his dreams at the Wedlock Creek Bar and Grill. She was shooting darts and almost hit him in the chest. Bull's-eye to the heart and that was that. We weren't a love match, anyway and only made out a few times—and badly. Zero chemistry. Oh, well."

"What about Liam's brother, Drake? He's gorgeous."

Norah nodded. "He is, but he's got it bad for someone."

"What? Liam never said a word! Who?"

Norah took another sip of coffee. "Oh, I'm not a hundred percent sure, but I've seen the way he looks at a certain someone. Mark my words, there's something brewing. Anyway, like I said, I've seen the way Liam looks at you. The man loves you. No doubt. Am I ever wrong? About anything? Wait—don't answer that. Just trust me."

"I love you," Shelby said, reaching to hug her younger sister.

"Ditto." She popped up from her chair, taking her

coffee with her. "Time to open up Treasures. Can't keep the Minnow sisters waiting."

Shelby smiled. Suddenly, a fussy wail came from the nursery. "Thank you for everything, Norah. I'll see you later." She saw her sister out, then headed to get Alexander. He looked a hundred percent better, his color great and he was clearly hungry.

At least she had one third of her heart right here with her.

Shane had just finished his applesauce, half of which seemed to end up on the baby's chin, when the doorbell rang.

Please be Shelby, he thought. He hated the way they'd left things. Hated the way he'd hurt her when that was the last thing he wanted to do—in fact, the very thing their marriage was supposed to protect them from.

But of course it wouldn't be Shelby. She had Alexander, freshly discharged from the clinic, and wasn't supposed to bring him over for a few days. At least the doctor had amended it from a week. And as Liam had said, he could use a few days apart from her, though it killed him to be separated from Alexander for even a day. He needed the time away from Shelby to reinforce his original plan for their marriage. Once he had all that as solid and settled in his head as it had been when he'd first proposed to her, he'd be good to go. Onward for the future for the good of their family.

It was looking at her that started problems.

Seeing her when she first woke up with those sleepy eyes and her sexy bed head and the way her long T-shirts and yoga pants clung to her curves.

Watching her scoop up the babies and smother them in morning kisses, her love for them shining in her eyes and in her every gesture.

And catching the way she'd look at him sometimes when she wasn't guarding herself.

Except he wasn't supposed to want her to look at him like that.

He shook his head to clear it, as if that ever worked, then plopped Shane in the playpen in the living room and headed to the door, sure it was yet another delicious delivery from the Pie Diner. The Ingalls women had stocked his fridge full of quiche, pot pies and fruit pies.

But it was his mother standing on the doorstep. "Just thought I'd pop by to see how you are. Lovely evening." She seemed to be trying to muster a smile but couldn't make it happen.

Larissa Mercer was a very private person and hid her emotions well, but Liam could plainly see she was a nervous wreck.

"You okay, Mom?" Liam held the door open wide, and his mother stepped inside, her heels clicking on the tile.

"Dad told me about your conversation," she said, taking off her jacket and folding it over her arm. She sat down on a tall-backed chair facing the fireplace. "I don't think I've ever seen him so emotional and lost for words at the same time."

Hmm. That was unexpected. Liam sat down across from her. "Did you know he was adopted?"

Larissa waited a beat. Talking about family secrets, talking about anything other than the weather or last night's dinner or their feelings in the most superficial manner, wasn't the Mercer way and he knew this had to be hard for his mom. "I've known since the day he proposed marriage to me. He broke down about it a couple of hours after I said yes. He told me he couldn't accept my hand in marriage unless I knew the whole truth about him—which was that he 'wasn't a real Mercer.'"

Once again, Liam was struck by the image of his father as a younger man, a man on one knee, proposing to the woman he loved—and refusing to lie to her. Refusing to go forward in life when she didn't know something he deemed fundamental about him.

That was character. And it gave him hope for his dad.

"I told him he absolutely was a real Mercer," his mother continued, "and that I'd love him the same no matter to whom he was born. I'll never forget his expression—he was so touched. But once I knew and he felt comfortable moving forward, he put the whole thing out of his mind. He never brought it up again."

His parents had been married for thirty-one years. They'd never talked about it again? Jeez. Talk about repression.

"That's no way to live," Liam said. "Blocking out the truth, pretending something isn't so."

Like his feelings for Shelby. How much he wanted her.

How much he loved her.

There it was. What he'd refused to admit to himself. He loved Shelby. So much. His love for her had come bursting out of every cell of his body without his control. Because like Shelby said, that was how love worked. You couldn't control it.

But you could control yourself. You could pretend. You could deny.

Like his father had.

Like Liam had to. To make sure all he cared about was protected.

Arrrgh! Why was this so hard? He'd had it all figured out. And then *wham*, blast to the center of his theory and the practice.

"No, it's no way to live," his mother said. "But it's what he needed to do. It was his business, so I never pressed him to talk about it. Maybe I should have."

"I understand why you didn't bring it up. He wanted it forgotten. And Dad can be difficult to talk to sometimes."

"No kidding," she said, finally smiling.

"I'm not sure I can forgive him for not visiting Alexander in the clinic. He was really sick. And Dad didn't come. That was the true test of his feelings for his grandson and he failed miserably."

"I know. And trust me, your father was tormented about it and still is. Right now your father is very wrapped up in how he *feels*, how he thinks things have to be. But there are consequences to his actions and we'll just have to see what happens."

How he thinks things have to be. Like Liam and his insistence that he and Shelby have a platonic marriage?

Consequences. Like losing Shelby, anyway?

He felt his heart sink along with his stomach. Arrgh again! *Focus on your dad and not yourself.*

"I'm not sure I want to watch," Liam said. "Family train wreck coming up next. Stay tuned."

"Well, whatever happens with your father, know that you and Shelby and Alexander and Shane have my full support. They are my grandsons. Both of them. They're my treasures. I've just known one a bit longer than the other."

Treasures. Like the name of Shelby's shop. Like Shelby. Pure treasure.

His mother stood and went over to say hello to Shane, scooping up the baby and giving him a cuddle. "I can't wait to get to know you more and more." She kissed his cheek, then put him back down. "I'll see you soon, Liam."

He walked his mother to the door, so damned twisted up about his marriage. How it was supposed to work. How it was supposed to last. Shouldn't he keep up the emotional and physical distance from his wife?

If so, why did that sound so incredibly stupid and impossible to his own ears?

Liam walked over to the wall of windows, looking out at the dark night, the woods dimly illuminated by the yard lights. A chill ran up the nape of his neck as a terrible thought came over him.

Maybe the answer was *no* marriage instead of a farce. All this time he'd thought they had to be married, legally wed, to have what they needed and wanted—both babies. But maybe it was better to live separate lives and share custody. Splitting the week. Splitting the babies. Not that that sounded like a good idea.

He didn't want Shane only half the week. He didn't want to give up Alexander half the time. He wanted them to grow up as brothers.

Which brought him back to being married to Shelby. Their mother.

Except living a lie was no longer acceptable. His

father had proven that. Harrington Mercer could live
with his head stuck in the sand all he wanted. But
Liam wouldn't. He and Shelby weren't a real husband
and wife. And pretending to be a family under a lie
like that was wrong. But living together as a real husband and wife in every sense of the word? No. Liam
knew that led to nothing but heartache down the road,
and would pit him and Shelby against each other. Love
didn't last. As least for him. And two little boys' lives
would be affected. Again.

He needed to sit down with Shelby and talk this
through, how they were going to deal with the situation.

Because he couldn't live like this.

Liam dropped off Shane with the Ingallses, who
doted over him and tried to push more pie on Liam.
At this rate, he'd be a thousand pounds in a month.
He thanked them for watching Shane for an hour or
two—however long it would take him and Shelby to
reach some kind of new arrangement—and headed
over to her apartment.

He rang the bell and when he heard her footsteps
coming down the stairs, his heart sped up.

He couldn't wait for her to open the door. He
couldn't wait to see her face. He couldn't wait to pull
her in his arms.

Because he loved her. So damned much he felt it in
his blood and veins and every beat of his heart.

What the hell? He'd come over here determined to
change things between them, to live truthfully.

*And the truth is that you love Shelby Ingalls Mer-
cer, your wife.*

That is the truth, the whole truth, so help you, God.

The door opened.

Shelby stood there, looking beautiful as always in her faded jeans and long-sleeved T-shirt, her wedding ring sparkling in the dim lighting of the vestibule on Alexander's back as she held him.

"Liam, is everything okay? Is Shane okay?"

"Shane is fine. I left him with your family for a bit. To come see you."

Her expression went from worried to alarmed.

Because she loves you, too, moron. It hit him like a ton of the old bricks. That was what she'd been trying to say earlier. She loved him. And always had.

He reached for her hands. "You were right about everything, Shelby."

"I was?" she said tentatively, putting her hands in his.

"About how love works. You can't control it. Try and you'll only end up with an ulcer."

She smiled. "I know. I've been popping antacids left and right."

"If we love each other, and it's clear as day that we do, we need to have a real marriage. Full of love and passion and give and take. Support. Loving, honoring, cherishing. In sickness and in health. For richer and for poorer, for as long as we both shall live."

"Oh, God, Liam. I do. I do!"

He laughed and pulled her into a hug. "And if we argue, and I'm sure we will, if we stomp off all angry at each other, we're strong enough to withstand it."

"You're right," said a deep voice from behind him. "Because we're Mercers. And that's what Mercers do."

Liam whirled around. His father stood inches away on the sidewalk.

"I'd like to see my grandson, if that's all right," Harrington said. He was holding a small bag in his hands. "I have something for him."

My grandson. Finally.

"Sure," Shelby said. "Come on up."

Liam walked up the stairs to Shelby's apartment and realized the usual hundred-pound weight was gone from each shoulder.

The moment his father entered the apartment he rushed toward Alexander in his playpen and lifted him up, tears in his eyes. "My grandson. My precious grandson. I'll never let you down again. I promise you that. I have something for you. Something that's yours." He reached into the bag and pulled the little brown cowboy hat he'd given Alexander the Friday that all their lives had changed.

"I've been looking all over for that," Liam said. "Glad you found it."

Harrington looked away for a moment, then square at Liam. He kissed Alexander on the cheek and then put him back down in the playpen. "I didn't find it. I took it back. The night you and Shelby told us about Alexander and Shane and the baby switch."

Oh, God. Dad.

"After you left the other day I sat looking at that tiny Stetson for hours," Harrington said. "Your mother tried to talk sense into me but I wouldn't listen. And finally I just kept thinking about lines from the letter. From my mother, Alexandra. From my father, Wilton. And from what Pearl said."

Shelby practically gasped. "You went to see Pearl?"

"Damned right, I did. I adopted two of her dogs, too."

Shelby laughed. "Really?"

Harrington nodded. "I named one Clint. Your mother gets naming rights for the second one. Young German shepherds mixed with God knows what."

"Good for you, Dad. You always wanted a dog. Now you'll have two."

"Two sons, two grandsons, two dogs," Harrington said. He looked from Liam to Shelby and back to Liam. "Son, I'm sorry I couldn't see my way through this until now. It took some serious soul-searching, I'll tell you that. But no matter how I feel about myself, Alexander is my grandson. I love the stuffing out of him."

"I know you do, Dad. It must have hurt like hell to withdraw from him."

"It did. And it'll never happen again."

Shelby hugged Harrington and he hugged her back tight.

"We're Mercers," Harrington said. "And we're Ingallses. And we're McCords."

"McCords?" Liam repeated.

"My birth mother," Harrington said. "Her name was Jeannie McCord."

Shelby smiled. "Well, hopefully we'll be blessed with more children. I want five, did I mention that, Liam?" She grinned at her husband then turned to Harrington. "How about we give our next born McCord as a middle name. In Jeannie's honor."

Tears shone in Harrington's eyes. "I'd like that."

"Me, too," Liam said, holding his wife's hand.

* * *

That night, Shelby lay in bed, Liam spooned against her back, his arms wrapped around her. A breeze fluttered through the bedroom windows and ruffled the sheet covering them, goose bumps covering Shelby's very naked body.

Making love with Liam was everything she'd dreamed it would be, everything she'd fantasized about.

She hadn't felt this happy since she'd held Shane for the first time in the Wedlock Creek Clinic. Since she'd held Alexander for the first time and felt in her heart—long before her head caught up—that she was his mother, too.

Liam stirred, his hand moving up to her hair, then down to her shoulder. "I could get used to this," he murmured.

"Oh, me, too," she said, turning over.

"I love you, Shelby Mercer."

"I love you back, Liam Mercer."

"And I love our family." He sat up and reached for the glass of champagne they'd had to celebrate their new status as a "real" husband and wife, every wonderful, messy moment life had to offer. He held the glass up. "To us and our family."

She sat up and clinked her glass with his. "To us and our family. Forever."

"Forever," she repeated and kissed him.

They put down their glasses and lay facing each other, Liam caressing her hair, Shelby trailing a finger across his sexy chest.

"Waaah!" came a little cry from the direction of the nursery.

"Waah!" came another. "Waah!"

"I think the first was the multiple known as Shane," Liam said.

"And the second was the multiple known as Alexander."

"Waaah!" the cry came louder. One of those *come get me this minute* kind of cries.

"I've got it," Shelby said, getting out of bed.

"*We've* got it," he said, scooping her up in his arms and carrying her to the nursery, kissing her along the way.

Epilogue

Some months later Liam, Shelby, Alexander and Shane sat in the county courthouse, listening to the family court judge talk about how nicely this whole baby switch thing had turned out. A family had been brought together.

Shelby heard sniffles behind her and turned around. The entire Ingalls crew was dabbing tissues under their eyes, Norah full out ugly-crying.

Shelby grinned at her very emotional younger sister. Norah was half-crying tears of joy and half-crying from being very hormonal.

Her single sister had just discovered she was pregnant…with triplets. According to Aunt Cheyenne, maybe just stepping foot into the Wedlock Creek Chapel could bring multiples into your life.

Shelby's attention was taken by Harrington Mercer,

who sat in the row across the aisle from the Ingallses, a giant stuffed kangaroo, complete with a baby kangaroo in its pouch, on the seat next to him. His wife and son and his cousin Clara sat on the other side of Harrington.

Finally, Shelby and Liam stood, each holding a baby, Alexander and Shane in matching little brown Stetsons.

"It's official," Liam said. "We're all Mercers."

"Real Mercers," Harrington whispered.

Liam smiled and squeezed Shelby's hand. She knew what that squeeze meant. That everything about their family—the Mercers, the Ingallses and Liam and Shelby's marriage—had been real from the get-go. It had just taken them a little while to realize it, to catch up to it. Head and heart, heart and head. Now they were in sync.

And they were off to the Ingalls-Mercer wedding reception 2.0, this time at the Mercer mansion, which Larissa had gone way overboard on preparing for the ceremony and reception. *Lavish* was her mother-in-law's favorite word. Fine with Shelby. This might be a very real marriage, but it felt like a dream to Shelby. A dream—and a legend—come true.

* * * * *

MILLS & BOON

Coming next month

RESCUING THE ROYAL RUNAWAY BRIDE
Ally Blake

"Look," Will said, stopping to clear his throat. "I'm heading towards court so I can give you a lift if you're heading in that direction. Or drop you…wherever it is you are going." On foot. Through muddy countryside. In what had probably been some pretty fancy shoes, considering the party dress that went with them. From what he had seen there was nothing for miles bar the village behind him, and the palace some distance ahead. "Were you heading to the wedding, then?"

It was a simple enough question, but the girl looked as if she'd been slapped. Laughter gone, colour gone, dark tears suddenly wobbled precariously in the corners of her eyes.

She recovered quickly, dashing a finger under each eye, sniffing and taking a careful step back. "No. No, thanks. I'm… I'll be fine. You go ahead. Thank you, though."

With that she lifted her dress, turned her back on him and picked her way across the road, slipping a little, tripping on her skirt more.

If the woman wanted to make her own way, dressed and shod as she was, then who was he to argue? He almost convinced himself too. Then he caught the moment she glanced towards the palace, hidden some-where on the other side of the trees, and decidedly changed tack so that she was heading in the absolute opposite direction.

And, like the snick of a well-oiled combination lock, everything suddenly clicked into place.

The dress with its layers of pink lace, voluminous skirt and hints of rose-gold thread throughout.

The pink train—was that what they called it?—was trailing in the mud behind her.

Will's gaze dropped to her left hand clenched around a handful of skirt. A humungous pink rock the size of a thumbnail in a thin rose-gold band glinted thereupon.

He'd ribbed Hugo enough through school when the guy had been forced to wear the sash of his country at formal events: pink and rose-gold—the colours of the Vallemontian banner.

Only one woman in the country would be wearing a gown in those colours today.

If Will wasn't mistaken, he'd nearly run down one Mercedes Gray Leonine.

Who—instead of spending her last moments as a single woman laughing with her bridesmaids and hugging her family before heading off to marry the estimable Prince Alessandro Hugo Giordano and become a princess of Vallemont—was making a desperate, muddy, shoeless run for the hills.

Perfect.

Continue reading
RESCUING THE ROYAL RUNAWAY BRIDE
Ally Blake

Available next month
www.millsandboon.co.uk

LET'S TALK
Romance

For exclusive extracts, competitions
and special offers, find us online:

f facebook.com/millsandboon

◉ @millsandboonuk

𝕏 @millsandboon

Or get in touch on 0844 844 1351*

For all the latest titles coming soon, visit
millsandboon.co.uk/nextmonth